THE NIMNAD

Louise and Mitchell Knowles

* * *

For Charlotte

* * *

About The Author

Louise Knowles from Kent along with her husband Mitchell, have finally got round to writing their first children's story. They have wanted to write this story for some considerable time but due to work and family commitments just haven't had the time to dedicate to it before. Having worked with children for many years Louise has a great empathy with young people and she and Mitchell have drawn on some personal experiences to help tell this intriguing and emotional story.

CONTENTS

ACHOO!

"Get down Buddy! Get down. OMG! You're such a jar get down! Stop climbing all over me.... get down!" moaned Lucy. He continued to climb the walls, racing round and round Lucy's bedroom as if he had gone mad. Puffing and panting and stopping every so often only to plaster Lucy's nose with his long wet tongue. Lucy reached out to the side of her bed and felt her way to a pink lamp that sat on her bedside table, flicked the switch and slowly peeled open her eyes to see what was going on. As she did so, she could just about make out Buddy's ghost like figure. He was now sitting on her bed staring down at her cuddly toys that she kept on the floor just beside her bed.

Lucy reached down to grab one of them and Buddy began to get even more excited! She was beginning to get fed up with his silly behaviour and just wanted to get back to sleep, when she had a very strange feeling. She realised that the cuddly toy she was holding felt much heavier than usual and as she turned her attentions from Buddy to the toy, she had the shock of her life! It suddenly blinked and sneezed all over her face! She let out a loud scream and hid under the duvet.

"OMG! OMG!" she shouted as her heart was beating so fast she could almost hear it.

After what seemed like forever, she eventually managed to calm herself down, but she just laid there in silence, not daring to move. Then suddenly out of the silence and darkness she heard.

"ACHOO, ACHOO!"

"OMG! What is that?" she thought. But, as afraid as she was, Lucy slowly peeled down her duvet and peeped over the top. There at the bottom of her bed looking straight back at her was a funny looking creature. It had two skinny brown flesh covered legs and a round body covered in the finest pink hair you've ever seen. A cute little face which had a a little brown pug nose and two big round crystal clear blue eyes that were staring straight at her. It was looking just as surprised as she was! Fascinated, she watched the little creature as it twitched its nose, closed its eyes and let out several loud sneezes.

"ACHOO, ACHOO, ACHOO!"

Buddy lay trembling underneath Lucy's bed. Suddenly even he was not so brave and eager to play anymore. He waited quietly, just letting out the occasional half hearted whine whilst he observed Lucy's reaction from his hideout. Only once Lucy's voice had reached a familiar pitch did he crawl out from underneath her bed and creep out of her bedroom to find some peace and quiet. Quietly with a quivering voice Lucy had said.

"What on earth are you?"

The little pink creature looked at Lucy, blinked his huge eyes and replied in a squeaky high pitched voice "I'm a Nimnad.... but you can't see me."

"What the....??!!" said Lucy, with a screwed up face and feeling a lot braver now.

He paused for a moment and said "Well at least you're not supposed to be able to see me. Oh crap, I'm going to be in so much trouble," he continued as he paced back and forth across Lucy's bed. "I'm supposed to be invisible to humans. ACHOO!" he sneezed again.

"What's a Nimnad?" Lucy asked, still with her face a little screwed up!

"I'm a Nimnad," he replied.

"Yeah – I heard that, but what IS a Nimnad?.......... And WHAT are you doing in MY bedroom?" she asked.

"I don't know?.......... I've never had to think about it before? We've always been here." He said beginning to sound a bit confused himself.

"WE'VE ALWAYS BEEN HERE?" copied Lucy. "What d'you mean 'WE?'...... There are more of you?" she asked.

"Yes," he said. "We're everywhere. If it wasn't for us there'd be no balance of luck. Good and bad luck wouldn't exist without us. In fact life would be very boring without us!" he raised his voice indignantly.

The little pink Nimnad then went on to explain how Nimnads have existed on the earth for as long as humans have. He told Lucy that the moment a baby is born into the world a Nimnad is also created at exactly the same time. But that they have never been seen because they are invisible to humans, well, that was up until now. He went on to explain how the sex of the baby determines the colour of the Nimnad. Baby boys create blue Nimnads and baby girls create pink ones.

"So YOU must be MY Nimnad because you're pink. Right?" said Lucy.

"Nooo," he replied. "Once we have been created we don't stay with you forever. The luck has to be balanced."

"I don't understand?" Lucy complained, looking very confused.

"Well it's simple really....... We're moving around all the time, we never stop moving. So, if a girl touches a pink Nimnad she will get some good luck, but if she touches a blue one she will get bad luck." He explained.

"Oh I see!" Lucy sighed with relief. "So if a boy touches a blue one he gets good luck, but if he touches a pink one he gets bad luck! Is that what you mean?" now Lucy was grinning all over her face.

"Yeeessss! That's it." Said the Nimnad. "That's how the luck is balanced around the world, and that's our job..... That's what we're here for!"
Phew!..........At that moment Nim was feeling just as relieved about having been able to successfully explain the reason for his existence, as Lucy was about having been able to understand it!

"You know you're not as stupid as you look Lucy." He said, looking a bit happier now.

"And you're sooo not funny," she answered as she glared at the Nimnad.

They continued to chat and he told Lucy how, since the beginning of time, people have associated blue as a boy's colour, and pink as a girl's, and that Nimnads are the reason why. He also explained that when a person comes into contact with a Nimnad, the Nimnad disappears and reappears somewhere else, but they never know exactly where they will reappear. Lucy listened very carefully to the Nimnad and then asked if the pink ones are girls and blue ones boys.

"We are neither. We are just Nimnads. We are full of luck. Not good, not bad. Just luck." It all seemed very weird to Lucy, and in her mind she had already decided that HER Nimnad was a boy, despite it having pink hair!

"So WHY can I see you?...... If you're supposed to be invisible then WHY can I see you?" she asked the little pink hairy creature that was looking at her quite oddly now.

"Why ME?" she asked again, with a puzzled expression on her face. "What's so special about me?"

"Oh so you think you're special do you? Just because you can see me doesn't make you special Lucy." Said the Nimnad.

"Oh WHATEVER!" replied Lucy, in a sarcastic voice. There was a moment of silence and then Lucy said. "How do you know my name?"

"Err, well, it's like this Lucy, you know I said we can't choose where we go? Well that's not strictly true. You see exceptions can be made."

"What do you mean exceptions?" she asked curiously.

"Ok, there is one Nimnad, he's the oldest, and in fact he's so old nobody knows exactly how old he is. Some Nimnads even say he's as old as time itself. We call him the Great Nimnad because he knows where all the Nimnads are in the world all of the time. He sent me to you."

"Ok, so why did he send you to me?" she asked.

"I don't know? You don't ask questions. If you're sent to someone, you just go. Anyway even if you did ask he wouldn't tell you."

"You're not keeping secrets from me are you?" Lucy asked.

"No we can't keep secrets and we can't tell lies, honest." Replied the Nimnad.

Lucy, who was now feeling very relaxed with the Nimnad somehow knew he was telling the truth. She swung her legs over the side of her bed and slowly got out. She wandered over to her window, pulled back the curtain and gazed out into the darkness of the most unusual night that she had ever experienced. As she took a few moments to try to understand, and even believe what was going on she became aware of a faint glow coming from beside her neighbour's garden shed. It was pink. There was a footpath that ran along the side of Lucy's house and she noticed a blue glow that appeared to be coming from two Nimnads.

"OMG! I can see more of you, this is so sick, but why haven't I seen Nimnads before?" she asked in astonishment.

"The thing is Lucy," replied the Nimnad. "You CAN see us now because you believe in us. Often people only believe in the things they can see, and because you can see me, you believe in me, and that's why you can now see all the Nimnads."

Lucy immediately dashed excitedly out of her room, past Buddy, who was now curled up in a ball on the landing floor at the top of the stairs, and into her mum and dad's room. She shook her mum awake and whispered.

"Mum, mum, there's something you need to see in my room."

"What's that love, can't it wait until the morning? I was just dropping off to sleep"

"Oh please mum it's really important," replied Lucy in a whispered voice.

"Ok but be quiet don't wake your dad up, he's got to be up early for work tomorrow." Lucy's mum got out of bed and followed her across the landing to her bedroom. It was so dark on the landing that she nearly tripped over Buddy as he lay there trying to sleep. Lucy closed the door behind them took a few paces towards her bed, stopped, held out her arm and pointed her finger towards the Nimnad.

"Look mum." She said.

"Look at what love?" her Mum enquired.

"Look. There. You must be able to see it mum!" Lucy replied in a raised voice.

"Lucy, what are you talking about love? I can't see anything on your bed." Mum yawned.

The Nimnad was standing at the foot of Lucy's bed shaking his head from side to side saying to himself,

"I do NOT believe this. She hasn't listened to a word I've said."

"Oh mum, please tell me you can see it?" Lucy pleaded with a sound of desperation in her voice.

"See what?" asked her mum, sounding a bit desperate herself now.

"That little pink fluffy thing on the end of my bed mum." Lucy pointed at it.

"It's no good Lucy," said the Nimnad. "She can't see me. It's just YOU. Only YOU can see me."

"No," said Lucy. "My mum MUST be able to see you. I want HER to see you too."

"Who are you talking to love? Are you sure you're feeling okay?" asked her mum.

"No, I'm not actually. You've GOT to be able to see him mum." With that Lucy grabbed her mum's arms and pulled her towards the end of her bed.

"LOOK mum, he's THERE!"
The Nimnad was waving frantically and shouting out.

"HELLO! HELLO! She can't see me!"
Lucy's mum smiled at her, leaned forward and started reaching out for whatever it was that she was supposed to be able to see. She thought that maybe Lucy was sleep talking and that if she went along with Lucy's request that it may settle her down and she'd fall back to sleep........ And mum could go back to bed! As she reached forward she passed her arm through the little creature and instantly POOF! In a puff of powder pink smoke he was gone!

"Oh mum, what did you do that for?" He's gone now!" said Lucy, becoming more frustrated than ever!

"Oh love, I've had enough of this. I'm going back to bed, I can't be doing with this silly stuff any longer."

"But look, there mum!" Lucy pointed out of her window down to the garden. "Look can't you see those little blue and pink creatures glowing? There's one in next door's garden by the shed and two in the alley?"

"No, I can't love, you've probably just been dreaming. Come on, get back into bed you've got school in the morning." Said Mum.

"I know........ You don't have to remind me."

The thought of school made Lucy feel sick. She was thirteen years old and going through the most terrible time of her life so far. She was being bullied by a girl called Beth and all her friends.

"Move bitch!" or, "get out of my way!" followed by sarcastic laughter and, "yeah! Who d'you think you are?"..........
"You got beef?" normally followed by a shove, had become a routine part of her school day and Lucy had, had enough.

These days Lucy was becoming almost reclusive and she didn't relish the thought of going anywhere much since she'd left the happy go lucky days of primary school behind her.

As Lucy's mum staggered back to her bedroom she wasn't so lucky this time and tripped over Buddy who jumped up in surprise turned tail and headed to the safety of Lucy's bedroom. Ah!.... You stupid dog buddy!" her mum shouted out in anger as she suddenly shot across the landing... Not that it was Buddy's fault or that he was stupid. After all he WAS a black dog in the dark, and her anger was really aimed at herself for not putting the light on. Buddy was a border collie cross, mostly black in colour but with some white bits. But the white bits couldn't be seen in the dark! He was a gentle, loving dog who merely wanted to be loved back that's all. As Lucy sat on her bed feeling disappointed that her mum had just thought she'd been dreaming she suddenly noticed a small pink glow on the floor down beside her bed. It got brighter, just like the glow of a light bulb when a dimmer switch is slowly turned on, and out from this glow the little Nimnad reappeared back in her room!

"Lucy," the Nimnad began. "Your mum can't see us because she doesn't believe, and she can't believe because she doesn't know."

"Well I didn't know, but I can see you?" replied an annoyed Lucy. "How did that happen?" she asked him.

"Like I was telling you Lucy. You have been chosen by the great Nimnad. He must think that you are pretty special, and for some reason, it just so happens that your dog can see me too..... Hmm... I don't think that bit was supposed to happen?" he said as he thought out loud.
Just then Buddy walked back into the room, and the Nimnad sneezed again.

"That's funny?" remarked Lucy. "You weren't sneezing at all just now?"

"ACHOO! ACHOO!" the Nimnad sneezed again.

"You must be allergic to something in my bedroom," said Lucy.

"But I don't know any Nimnads that are allergic to anything Lucy," he said.

"So... Anyway. Are you my very own lucky Nimnad? You must be as you said you have been chosen for me?.. I think I should try you out now!" said Lucy.

"Try me out? What do you mean try me out? What do you mean?" he asked her, getting very agitated.

"I think it's time I got myself some luck, you don't mind do you? After all, you are here just for me, and I need as much luck as I can get if I'm going to school tomorrow." She said.

"Oh I see Lucy, but remember, once you touch me I'll disappear and you won't be able to see me for a while, so think carefully before you do." The Nimnad cautioned her. Lucy thought for all of FIVE seconds and decided she definitely needed all the luck she could get if she was to stand up to the bullies at her school that kept picking on her. She took one step forward and as she took another expecting to walk straight through the Nimnad she felt a hard thud on the end of her toes.

"OUCH!!" she shouted, as the poor little Nimnad flew off the floor, hit the back of the toy box lid and fell into the box. Bang! Down crashed the lid and the Nimnad was shut in. The room was silent for a moment. Then from inside the box Lucy heard.

"I've gone all dizzy and my head feels funny! I can't get out of this box! get me out! get me out of here!..... Pleeeeze!" Lucy went over to her toy box and gently lifted the lid.

"ACHOO!" went the Nimnad again. "I'm so sorry Nim I didn't mean to do that! is it ok if I call you Nim?"

"Yeah, WHATEVER! i don't mind." He replied as he rubbed his head with his little hands. She reached in and carefully lifted the Nimnad out of the box. Buddy, who by now, was looking rather confused by the strange goings on in Lucy's room wandered out of her bedroom and back on to the landing. The strange thing was that as Buddy left the room, Lucy suddenly lost touch of the Nimnad. He wasn't solid anymore and Lucy was fumbling around trying to keep him in her grasp and not let him fall to the floor. She could see him but she just couldn't feel him. She began to get upset and started to cry as emotion and confusion filled her head. At the sound of Lucy crying, Buddy came straight back into her room, and as he did so, a familiar sound filled the air again.

"ACHOO!" the Nimnad sneezed again, and all of a sudden Lucy was able to grab hold of him and cuddle him in her arms.

"It's Buddy! You must be allergic to Buddy! Every time he's in the room you become solid and start to sneeze!" she shouted out. That was it, enough was enough... Lucy's mum called out, "will you stop making so much noise and get to sleep!"

"Sorry mum!" called Lucy. "I'd better put the light out and get to sleep soon," she whispered.

"Yeah, that sounds like a good idea and you'd better keep your dog away from me in future, coz if that's what being human feels like you can keep it."

"SORREE!" replied Lucy "It's not my fault."
They both laid there in an awkward silence until they fell asleep.

AN UNEXPECTED CALL

Get up! Get up! Get up! Get up!! GET UP!!!! came the sound of Lucy's voice.

"Alright! give me a chance!" Nim shouted back.

"It's not me," Lucy giggled. "It's my alarm on my mobile." She explained.

"Well it blimmin well sounds like you." He said, still looking a bit annoyed.

"Yeah I know. That's because it IS me." She whined at him. "But I didn't just say it then. It was a recorded message that I put on my phone ages ago, lol!" she was laughing at his confusion. Then she remembered, "oh crap its school today. I reeeally don't want to go." And she started to feel sick.

The Nimnad, now wide awake jumped up. "Come on, get up and get ready.... You don't have to go alone today, I'm coming with you." He said with a big smile and wide awake crystal blue eyes that blinked as he spoke to her. She got dressed into her school uniform and looked in the mirror as she brushed her shoulder length straight blonde hair. She was of average height and had a pretty face, but the sight of herself ready for school filled her with a sense of dread. For even the sheer sight of herself in these clothes told her that she wasn't going to have a good day, for a day of wearing these clothes could only mean she would be at school, and for Lucy, school meant only one thing, misery. She used to like going to school but nowadays it was a very different story. Secondary school was not proving to be a very enjoyable experience for Lucy at all. From the moment she walked into her new classroom on the first day that she started, she'd had a feeling of impending doom, and for Lucy that feeling was proving itself to be correct on a daily basis. She had found herself to be quite alone and feeling very isolated having been separated from any of the familiar faces from her primary school... She didn't feel that she could relate to any of the girls in her class and they sensed it. Her bedroom had become her safe haven. A place where she could relax and a place where she didn't have to watch over her shoulder or worry about what anyone thought about her.

"Right," she thought. "Downstairs, tea and toast and then I'd better get going before I change my mind." Lucy frequently changed her mind on exiting the front door, and if she could get away with it she would go back upstairs, shut herself away in her room and disappear into a world of xbox games all day. Anything was better than facing up to the reality and harshness of her school life.

She went downstairs and into the kitchen to find her mum standing at the breakfast bar eating some cornflakes, and her dad was hovering over the gas hob waiting for some water to boil for a poached egg. Her mum was quite short and round with a very friendly face that nearly always had a welcoming smile on it. She had shortish blonde hair that just rested on her shoulders and fell in soft curls. She was never short of a cuddle if one was needed and always had time to listen to anyone who needed a listening ear. Dad, on the other hand, was taller than Lucy's mum. He could come across as a bit stern at times, but was much softer on the inside than he appeared on the outside........... A bit like a minstrel! He had a shiny bald head with a very thin lining of dark hair that hung along each side of his head like a pair of stage curtains. Ryan, Lucy's brother, had already had some cereal and gone to catch his bus. Lucy liked to put off the evil moment of leaving the house for as long as she possibly could.

She was just buttering some toast when the phone rang. "Can you get it love?" her mum shouted out from the front room where she was standing at the window, watching Ryan walk down the road.
Lucy put her knife down and answered the phone.

"Good morning, can I speak to Mrs Louise Miles please?" asked a very polite lady in a soft voice. "Yes who's calling please?" Lucy and her brother had always been told to ask who was calling when answering the phone on behalf of her mum and dad, probably so they could say they were out if they didn't want to speak to whoever was on the phone!

"GM TV" was the reply.
"Mum, it's the TV people for you!" shouted Lucy.

"Ok just coming love!" replied mum.
Lucy put the phone down on the worktop and finished buttering her toast. Her mum picked up the phone and said in her best telephone voice.

"Hello, Louise speaking."
After a short pause, Lucy heard, "I can't believe it, that's

fantastic..... I don't know what to say. Thank you so much. I've never won anything before."

"What mum?" Lucy asked her mum with a sound of urgency in her voice.

"I've won the GM TV prize!" her mum shrieked as she jumped up and down, clapping her hands together.

"OMG! what have you won mum?" Lucy was finding it hard not to get excited now, even though she didn't know why!

"TEN THOUSAND POUNDS!!" came an excited response from her mum, who by now had calmed down, but her eyes looked big and were wildly staring into space...................she was probably imagining what to spend it on.

"OMG!!!.............Mum! what're you gonna spend it on?"
Mum shook her head and blinked quickly. "I don't know?"
By now dad was joining in the euphoria as he shovelled his poached eggs on toast in to his mouth as quickly as he could.

"A BLIMMIN GOOD HOLIDAY!" he said with a raised voice and a mouthful of egg.
Mum began to raise her voice again.

"OOH YEAH!" she shouted.

"Can I get a new mobile now?" asked Lucy as she hugged her mum and the three of them started dancing round the kitchen.

Once they'd all calmed down, discussed what they were going to spend the money on and normality had returned, Lucy thought of Nim. She started looking around for him and there, sitting on the edge of the chair all wide eyed and with an all knowing, very wise looking smile on his face...... was the Nimnad. Lucy gasped with surprise and was just about to speak to him when he clenched his little fist and gently placed one out stretched finger on his lips, winked at Lucy and beckoned in a way as if to suggest that it was time to leave for school. There would be plenty of time to talk on the way. Lucy grabbed her blazer and school bag, gave her mum and dad a Kiss and called out "Love you loads!" then left the house.

TO SCHOOL AND BACK

As Lucy walked along, the Nimnad ran alongside her trying to keep up.

"Come on Nim, I'll be late if we don't get a move on. Can you believe mum won all that money? she's so lucky." She bent down and went to pick him up, but her outstretched arms passed right through him! Lucy had forgotten the rule about him disappearing every time she touched him when Buddy wasn't around! There was a puff of pink smoke and he was gone!

"Oh, no! I forgot that would happen," thought Lucy as she stomped off down the road on her way to school. She felt sick to her stomach at the thought of going alone without the support of her new companion.

It had not yet occurred to Lucy that by passing her arms through the Nimnad she had just earned herself her first bit of good luck. As Lucy walked along the road she spotted a pink glow hovering just above someone's gate post, and as she got closer she could see the Nimnad appearing from within the glow! He jumped onto Lucy's school bag, clung on tight and off they went.

"Oh I'm sooo glad you turned up again when you did, I was missing you already." Lucy said with a sigh of relief. "I forgot you'd disappear if I touched you."

"That's ok. It must be your lucky day." The Nimnad said, with a nod and a wink. Lucy continued along the road. It was a straight journey most of the way to school. It was mostly along a main road with quite a lot of traffic running through it. As Lucy approached the main road, having walked along a fairly lengthy residential road from where she lived, she would first pass the big church where she was christened as a baby, and before that, where her mum and dad were married. That Church sat beside a grassy area which housed a swing park. Lucy used to play there when she was younger on her way home from school with her friends. Her mum would stop off in there if the weather was fine, sometimes taking a snack and something to drink as well. Unfortunately this was now a place that Lucy avoided due to the fact that she had fallen victim to some rather more unpleasant experiences in that same place during the past couple of years. Anyway, past the Church the road was lined with very big houses that sat back quite far from the pavement and those houses that didn't sit back so far had big front gardens. Some of them had wrought iron gates shutting them off from uninvited visitors. Lucy always thought that those houses looked quite posh. The road continued like that for about a mile and then came the entrance to the woods. Lucy always walked quickly past there because she would get a tingling down her spine and the hairs on the back of her neck would stand up. She always used to imagine that someone or something might grab her and pull her into the woods if she didn't get past quick enough! Then there were more houses, smaller houses now not quite as grand as the others further back up the road. Some were old cottages with front doors that opened straight onto the pavement with no front garden at all. Lucy always thought that she would worry if she lived in one of those for fear that someone might bang on the window as they walked past. She would then pass over a small arched brick built bridge which if she stopped and looked over the side she could see a small river running underneath it. A little way further down the road there was a parade of shops.......... a post office, chemist, small Co-op supermarket, that kind of thing. Not much further along was Lucy's school. All in all it used to take her about an hour to get to school because she was too afraid to go by bus due to the fact that one of Beth's mates thought it was funny to set the back of Lucy's hair on fire when sitting behind her on the way home from school one day! Lucy's mum had been to school and made a complaint about the bullying but as usual, not much came of it. So Lucy had made a conscious decision............. From that moment on, she would never travel alone on the bus again, and seeing as though there wasn't anybody else who travelled her way to school, meaning, someone she felt she could call on for company, she always walked. Rain or shine, she always walked there and back alone. That was until now......... Because now she had a little friend all of her own to relieve the loneliness!

As Lucy arrived at the parade of shops, she reached into her pocket for some money. She had planned to pop into the Co-op to buy herself a drink to go with her packed lunch, but as she approached the shop, five girls came out of the door one after the other. Lucy's stomach instantly knotted up and the palms of her hands became clammy. She felt clumsy and inadequate and didn't know where to look. The five girls descending onto the pavement only a few metres in front of Lucy were largely responsible for making her experience at Secondary School very unpleasant. Lucy discretely put the money back in to her pocket, crossed the road and pretended that she hadn't seen them. She walked briskly along with her head held low and her eyes fixed on her feet, not daring to look up in case she came into eye contact with one of the girls. For that would definitely start an episode of taunting and name calling coming her way.

These girls were in the same year as Lucy at school and were apparently part of the 'popular' crowd, although if popular meant being big headed, obnoxious and self centred I'm not too sure that being popular was all it was cracked up to be! Anyway the group of girls in question were a selection of all shapes and sizes. One of them was called Kerry Kristian, she was quite tall with long straight blonde hair. She was of slim build and quite attractive, but oh boy did she know it! Then there was Amber Hibbard who was responsible for Lucy walking to school. She also had blonde hair but she had hers in a short straight bob style and she wasn't as tall as Kerry. In fact she was rather on the short side herself, quite petite in fact and rather tomboyish. Justine Jackson and Carley Campbell, now they seemed to be joined at the hip. Always wearing the same clothes as each other and when one had a new bag or shoes, the other would go out and copy the same. Neither of them minded they just enjoyed being the same.

Justin was of medium build and average height for her age and she had dark brown hair, shoulder length in a curly perm style. Carley was about the same height as Justin but of larger frame and yes......, she also had shoulder length dark brown hair in a curly perm style! Last but not least was Beth Mackenzie. Now, SHE was the ringleader. Quite big built with long mousy brown wavy hair, which she nearly always wore up in a ponytail and would wear so much fake tan that if she were anyone else......... she would have the mickey taken out of her! Oh no... Not Beth.... Nobody would dare! She had a reputation which preceded her, and that was that she was apparently a really nasty piece of work, and that nobody would want to mess with her for fear of being punched in the face. Even though there didn't seem to be any one that had actually seen her in action, her reputation seemed to be enough to create a feeling of fear around her. Although they all looked quite different in one way or another, they all had one very big thing in common and that was that they were very unpleasant, thoughtless, intimidating girls of a quite destructive nature. Further down the road Lucy had no alternative but to cross back over onto the same side as her school, as she was nearly there. Unfortunately this also meant that she was going to come face to face with the Mackenzie mob. Again Lucy's stomach tied up in knots, she only hoped that she could make it into the school gates before they started on her. Luckily she managed to mingle into the crowd of latecomers who were all rushing to their classrooms before the bell went and made it safely to her classroom in one piece. Once Lucy was comfortably seated at her desk she didn't look left or right. She just stared straight ahead whilst waiting for Mr Watson to call the register.

"Right then!" shouted Mr Watson. "Girls be quiet now!.... I need to call the register so that all you lovely ladies can get to your first lesson of the day, I'm sure you can't wait." He said sarcastically. The noise turned to silence and Mr Watson began to call out names. As Lucy sat at her desk waiting for her name to be called she spotted a ten- pound-note folded in half on the floor at the front of the classroom. She couldn't believe it was just lying there in full view of everyone but nobody else seemed to have noticed it. Her eyes widened and she had a strong urge to get up from her desk to go and pick it up, but that would look too obvious she thought and maybe somebody would claim it if they saw her pick it up?

"That's two weeks pocket money!" Lucy thought. She waited in anticipation for the class to be dismissed.

"Ok girls," said Mr Watson as the first bell rang. "Off you go! Get to your first lesson as quickly as you can!"
Lucy watched in disbelief as everybody stepped over, on or past the ten-pound note without noticing it! At last! Lucy managed to manoeuvre from behind her desk to the front of the classroom where the note was still lying on the floor. She accidentally on purpose dropped her bag, and as she bent down to pick it up she grabbed the money at the same time. This was her lucky day, what a great start!
"How come I was the only one that saw it?" she thought.

"Lucky me!" she told herself and proceeded out of the classroom and down the corridor toward her next lesson.

"Wait for me Lucy!" Nim called after her.

"Have you forgotten about me already?" he continued to call after her as she hurried off down the corridor.

"No of course not, but I couldn't see you and I had my eyes on that money. Did you see it? I couldn't believe that no else saw it?"

"Well," said Nim. "You touched me didn't you? I'm not just a pretty face you know Lucy."
Just then Mr Watson walked briskly past them as they were dawdling along talking to each other.

"Lucy Miles, stop mumbling to yourself and get to your next lesson. Otherwise I can see you coming back for detention young lady." He said in a very pompous manner.

Mr Watson was a very tall, very slim built man with fine sandy colour hair, cut short and parted on one side. He wore gold rimmed glasses which were of an oval sort of shape and always wore a very smart grey suit and tie with a crisp white shirt.

"Eeuwww! shall we call her MUMBLER from now on?" a familiar voice called out from behind her.
"Or should we just call her geek as usual?" asked another.

"I don't know? what shall we call you today Lucy?" asked Carley as she ran up alongside her. It was the Mackenzie mob.

"Are they the same girls we saw at the shops this morning Lucy? don't they like you?" Nim wanted to know.

"Just don't talk to me Nim." Lucy gritted her teeth.

"They don't need an excuse to make my life a misery. They do it for fun, and if they think I'm talking to myself I'll have had it for good." She whispered under her breath with her head held low whilst picking up her pace so as to get to Maths class as quickly as possible. The little pink Nimnad jogged along beside her. She could hear the girls laughing and making fun of her as she hurried away from them. Lucy reached her classroom after what seemed like an eternity, but in actual fact it was only about a three minute walk. She entered the room and made her way over to her desk. She had whispered to Nim on the way in to keep very close to her, because she didn't want anyone else to touch him. She was starting to feel a certain kind of ownership over the Nimnad and wanted to keep him to herself. The teacher hadn't arrived to start the lesson and so there was a lot of noise going on in the classroom. Girls were chatting, laughing, some were even shouting across the room to each other. Lucy approached her desk, slipped between it and her chair and went to sit down. As she did so one of the girls sitting behind her pulled her chair away, leaving Lucy to fall backwards, landing flat on the floor on her bum. Poor Lucy, her face was bright red and she felt sick with embarrassment. The whole class was laughing at her and she felt like she wanted to cry. She clambered to her feet and began looking around for her little pink Nimnad to see if he was ok, but he was nowhere to be seen. Just at that moment Mr Hinchcliffe walked into the classroom. The madness of the room and the noise of the laughter changed in an instance, to silence.

All of the girls were afraid of upsetting Mr Hinchcliffe because he had one of the loudest, deepest voices you have probably ever heard and when he got cross and shouted, no-one dared to breathe let alone misbehave.

"What's been going on in here whilst you've been waiting for me?" he bellowed.

"I've just had a complaint from Madame Boisson and she's six classes down the corridor!" he bellowed again in his deep foghorn voice.

"Now sort yourselves out and get seated at your desks! I've got the results of last week's test.... AND THEY'RE NOT VERY IMPRESSIVE!" he finished what he was saying with a very disgruntled look on his face. Everyone sat down very quietly and waited in trepidation to hear their name called out, followed by their test result.

Lucy was dreading it because maths was one of her weakest subjects at school. She had missed so many lessons during the past two years that she had fallen behind with a lot of her work and consequently her confidence had fallen dramatically as well. She was too embarrassed to put her hand up and ask the teacher for help in case anyone laughed at her and said she was stupid, which the bullies frequently did anyway. The trouble was, the more she didn't ask for help, the further behind she fell. Lucy was actually a fairly bright girl but because of the situation at school with the other girls, it wasn't showing in her work. Quite often her mind would go blank if a teacher spoke to her or asked her a question, especially in front of the class, and to all intents and purposes it would seem as though Lucy had no knowledge of anything in her brain! When, if the truth be told there was actually more stored in Lucy's brain than some of the other girls, but the shutters would come down and that would be that. Poor Lucy wouldn't be able to let it out. She called it brain freeze.

Mr Hinchcliffe was quite a short chubby man, who had a very powerful personality. He had a mop of curly auburn hair and a chunky moustache that was slightly greying around the edges.

He usually wore a brown suit, and always wore a shirt and tie, neither of which matched each other. He always wore comfy looking brown suede shoes and carried a soft leather briefcase.

The Nimnad, by now, had appeared on the other side of the classroom door. He was on the outside looking in and was hanging on to the door handle with one hand, whilst frantically waving at Lucy with the other as he peered through the door window.

"Just stay there." Lucy mouthed.

She figured that if he stayed there, then at the end of the lesson when the door was opened he would be on the other side and no one else would get to touch him. Then she would be able to collect him on the way out!

Back to the test results! Believe it or not the top girl in the class was usually Carley Campbell. Yes remember?....... One of the terrible twins? The two girls that always like to dress the same as each other who are part of the Mackenzie mob? There were two of that lot who were in Lucy's Maths class and they were Carley Campbell and Amber Hibbard. They always sat next to each other behind Lucy in Maths. In fact it was Amber who had pulled Lucy's chair from under her. Lucy was bound to be bottom of the class or if not, nearly bottom. Mr Hinchcliff began. He started with the lowest first. Lucy's brain started turning to mush as she waited to hear her name, but only three names into the list came the announcement of Carley Campbell's name with 27%!

"What the......?" thought Lucy to herself.
She was thinking that this couldn't be right. Carley was really good at Maths. Lucy turned to look at Carley, whose face was one of shock and embarrassment. One by one Mr Hinchcliff continued to call out the names. The marks were getting higher and higher but still no Lucy. She was just beginning to think that she must have scored 0% when Mr Hinchcliff announced,

"Lucy Miles – 93%!"

"What? how can that be right?" she pondered to herself as she looked around at the other girls in the class. She could see that most of them had a look of confusion on their faces too, for this was not as normal. Something weird was going on! Mr Hinchcliffe, who also appeared to be rather confused, paused for a moment, raised his eyes to briefly glance around the classroom, and then carried on with the last few names. The only explanation Lucy could think of was that somehow, hers and Carley's, who by the way looked completely fed up, and she wasn't used to feeling that way about ANYTHING, results must have got mixed up on the computer system. When the end of the lesson came Lucy left her desk and made a dash for the door. She opened it, beckoned to the Nimnad and dashed to the toilets so she could speak to him in private. As soon as Lucy reached the toilets she glanced around to check that no-one was watching, crouched down, and placed her open bag on the floor and Nim jumped in. Then she picked the bag up in her arms, being very careful not to touch him for fear that he would disappear again! She then hurried into the toilets and locked herself and the little pink Nimnad inside one of the cubicles.

"What was all that about Nim?" she whispered. "What's going on? something very weird just happened." The little pink Nimnad, was staring up at Lucy from where he was now standing on the closed toilet seat

"I'm finding it difficult to take everything in today... I mean first of all I woke up in the middle of the night to find you in my bedroom and as if THAT wasn't weird enough all of this good stuff keeps happening. I'm not used to so much good stuff, and how could I get 93% for a Maths test? it's impossible. I'm no good at Maths!" Lucy began to raise her voice a little.

"There are going to be some big changes in your life Lucy. That's why I'm here for you, to help you make them. You'll get used to me being around soon enough and the Maths... well that's because you landed on me when you fell over, remember?"
He gazed into Lucy's eyes with his big blue eyes as they

blinked. "Touch a pink Nimnad and you get good luck? Well your good luck must have been the mix up on the computer Lucy." He looked at her with the sweetest little smile on his face.

The bell sounded to tell everyone that it was time to go to the next lesson. French was next on the agenda and was largely uneventful, as was the rest of the school day. Lucy had just plodded through as best she could manage and the little pink Nimnad stayed close by her.

Finally the bell was sounding for home time and Lucy tried to make her way out of school as quickly as she could, in order to miss another confrontation with the McKenzie mob. As she made her quick exit out of the building she could see that it had been raining again and so she took her umbrella out of her bag ready in case it was needed. It was gently drizzling with rain, not heavy but enough to get you wet through if you were in it for long enough, so she put her umbrella up and started towards the school gate.

There was such a large crowd of girls all trying to push their way through the opening of the gate at once that Lucy lost sight of Nim for a moment and another girl passed right through him with her leg! Oh no! POOF! There was a small cloud of pink smoke and he was gone! Lucy had a sense of loneliness now. She had got used to him being around and didn't like how she felt when he wasn't there. She watched the girl and slowly followed along behind her to see what would happen next. The girl stopped at the bus stop with her friend to wait for her bus home. A few moments later the girl's mobile phone rang and she answered it.

"Yes, hello that's me," she said. "Wow you're joking, I can't believe it, that's great. Thank you, bye."
The girl turned to her friend and said. "You know that competition I entered in 'Bliss' to win tickets to go and see One Direction?"

"Yeah?" replied her friend.
Well I've won! My names just been picked in the draw!" she got louder and more excited as she spoke.

"That is SO not fair," thought Lucy. "She's stolen some of my good luck! Nim is MINE. I hope I find him soon."

Lucy felt a surge of jealousy run through her. She wandered off down the road to make her way home. She could see Beth and her friends hanging around by the parade of shops so she decided to cut around the back, through the alley that ran behind them, and come out at the other end so that she would miss them. Unfortunately she'd been spotted already, and the mob had doubled back and followed her down the alley. She sensed them behind her and quickened her pace. She began to feel frightened and wished that Nim was with her. As Lucy hurried along, she could hear the footsteps of the girls behind her getting faster and the girls began to shout out.

"BITCH!!.. When we get you we're gonna bang you up!"
Lucy's tummy started to tighten up in a big knot and she started to run. Still holding her umbrella up to shield her from the rain, and trying to dodge the puddles, Lucy ran as quickly as she could. There was a tight bend coming up ahead and

then the alley would open back onto the pavement at the other end of the parade. She slowed down a little as she manoeuvred round the bend so as not to slip over on the wet gravely ground. Just at that moment a familiar voice came from closely behind her!

"Watch out Lucy, there's a blue Nimnad up in front...., look out!"

Lucy looked round instead of where she was going, to see where the voice was coming from, and her little pink Nimnad was hanging from the framework inside her umbrella! She was so pleased to see him!

"Don't go through the blue ones! Remember Lucy?" Nim shouted out. In an instant Lucy had an idea. Still running, she looked round and past Nim to see how close the mob was, and they were pretty close! She slowed her pace down a little, waited for them to get a bit closer, and then sped up again. Lucy dodged around the blue Nimnad, but the gang of girls couldn't see it so they ran straight on, Beth was in front so she caught it full on! There was a puff of blue smoke and the blue Nimnad was gone! Lucy picked up her pace again now as they were getting closer and closer! They were calling out threats of what they would do to her when they caught her. She turned right at the end of the alley and continued running towards home. As the mob ran out of the alley after her, a big white delivery van drove into the parking bay at the front of the shops. He pulled in at quite a speed, due to the fact that he wasn't paying enough attention to his driving because he was slightly lost and was trying to read the address on his delivery note at the same time. The van clipped the curb and skimmed right along the edge of a large puddle, which in turn splashed up like a mini tidal wave and showered dirty water all over Beth! She just stood there, dripping from head to toe! For a few seconds Lucy and Beth stared at each other.

"That'll teach the BITCH!!" Thought Lucy. Then she turned and started running again, as quickly as she could towards home.

Beth's voice could be heard shouting.

"YOU'RE DEAD!!

No more was to come of the chase, at least for now... It was over. A relieved Lucy walked along with what felt like her best friend in the world right now, her little pink Nim.

It was a calm and quiet walk home, Lucy and the Nimnad were a bit weary from their ordeal and neither of them had much to say, so they didn't say anything at all to each other all the way home. They just felt a certain kind of comfort being around each other. They were getting to know each other and it felt nice.

When they reached Lucy's house she took her front door key out of her bag where she kept it in a little zip up pocket on the front. Before Lucy had even put her key in the lock Buddy was the other side barking and jumping around impatiently. She opened the door and the Nimnad jumped backwards as Buddy pounced at Lucy and jumped up to her in search of acknowledgement , which she did so immediately of course with a cuddle and a stroke. Planting a big kiss on top of his head she said, "come on Buddy, that's enough. Go in now." To which he turned tail and walked indoors.

"ACHOO! not again." Said Nim.

Lucy looked at him sympathetically and smiled, and then the three of them went straight upstairs to Lucy's room. She put her bag down and took her blazer off.

"Thanks for helping me on the way home, I don't know what I would have done if you hadn't have turned up when you did."

She decided to take advantage of Nim's allergic reaction to Buddy and she bent down and put her arms around the little pink Nimnad and gave him a kiss on the cheek.

"Oh thank you Lucy." Nim replied as a waft of affection engulfed him. It was a feeling that he would get used to over the coming weeks. It was not only Lucy who's world had changed dramatically over the past couple of days, but the little pink Nimnad had entered a whole new world too. He was not used to all this human contact and he was beginning to experience what it was like to feel human emotions. His assignment to Lucy was going to have a profound effect on him for the rest of his life.

"Lucy! Is that you?" mum called out from the kitchen.

"ACHOO!" the little pink Nimnad let out a very loud sneeze.

"Bless you!" her mum called up the stairs.

"Thanks mum!" Lucy replied as she tried not to laugh. "I'll be down in a second!" she continued.

"Come on Nim, I'd better go down and see my mum. She won't believe it when I tell her what happened on the way home today."

"Well she won't believe it if you tell her about me being there," said the Nimnad. "You'd better leave me out of it otherwise your mum will think you're making it all up, ok?"

"deffo," said Lucy. "It's so frustrating to have such a cool friend like you, and not be able tell anyone though."

"I know Lucy but never mind," said the Nimnad. "I'm here for you and that's the most important thing isn't it?"

"Lucy! Are you coming down then?" called her mum impatiently. "Yes mum, I'm coming now!" Lucy danced down the stairs and went into the kitchen. Her mum was standing at the sink washing up the breakfast things. That was usually the first thing Lucy's mum did when she got home from work. She would take her coat off, pull up her sleeves and get stuck in. Everyone was always in such a hurry in the mornings that it would all get left where it was and as mum was the first one home she would have the pleasure of tackling it.

"Are you going to get yourself a drink and a bite to eat Lucy? dinner won't be ready until about 7.00pm tonight. I need to go shopping first." Her mum said as she vigorously rubbed Weetabix from a breakfast bowl.

"Ok mum, can I have one of those chocolate cookies with a cup of tea then?" asked Lucy " Yes that's fine love, make me a cuppa whilst you're there would you?" mum asked, giving Lucy one of her loving smiles.
Whilst Lucy was waiting for the kettle to boil she began to tell her mum all about her journey home from school, leaving out the part about the Nimnad of course! her mum listened attentively as Lucy told her all about the chase down the alley and Beth getting soaked by the puddle.

"Good for you love," said her mum. "Don't let those girls get to you. Rise above their stupid behaviour and they'll leave you alone."

Anyway a little later on, Lucy went up to her room with the Nimnad and her mum went shopping. The Nimnad sat on the carpet next to Lucy staring straight ahead at the television screen. She was playing the Sims on her Xbox.

"Lucy! Do you want to come for a ride with me to Asda? Mum forgot to buy the spaghetti for dinner tonight so I'm going to get it now!" dad shouted up the stairs.

"Erm, ok then!" shouted Lucy, still gazing at the screen on her TV.

"Yes!" thought Nim. Anything's better than this."
Not much conversation had been exchanged between Lucy and her little friend whilst she had been playing her game and he couldn't wait to go out with Lucy and her dad as he had become quite bored. Boredom was not something that the Nimnad had ever experienced before. Until now his existence had been one of a calm serenity on another dimension, just gently hovering around dispatching luck to who ever came his way. But now things were very different, for he too was beginning to raise his expectations of his life. He would have to be very careful that he did not begin to enjoy the emotional feelings of humans too much, as it would be very difficult to say goodbye to Lucy when his task was done otherwise. The little pink Nimnad was beginning to grow very fond of Lucy, and he was very much looking forward to going out in Lucy's dad's car. He had never been in a car before!

AT THE SUPERMARKET

Lucy went downstairs, swiftly followed by the Nimnad. Mum was in the kitchen cooking up a delicious bolognaise sauce, and Buddy was curled up on his bed in the corner of the kitchen. He had grown accustomed to the new lodger by now and simply opened one eye, looked at the Nimnad, closed his eye again and went back to sleep.

"Come on then dad, shall we go?" Lucy said, as she stood by the living room door. Her dad was in the living room listening to the newsreader on the TV.

"Did you hear that?" he asked. "One in ten children will suffer bullying at school these days."

"Really? that's awful." Mum said with a frown on her face.

"Your not being bullied Lucy, are you?" her dad asked.

"What? Me? No.......... Of course not."

"That's good to know love, couldn't imagine you being bullied."

"They wouldn't dare dad." Lucy replied as she turned her head away. She could feel her eyes filling up and she didn't want her dad to see this. She would be really embarrassed if her parents knew what was happening to her at school.

"Ok then, let's get going," laughed dad, and they left the house.

The family car was a dark green Ford Mondeo Estate. Dad loved it because he could fit almost anything he needed to in the back, mum put up with it for the sake of dad, and

Lucy and her brother hated it. They used to call it 'THE LONG GREEN THING'.

Lucy would complain that it was too ugly and that she felt embarrassed when her mum or dad would pick her up or drop her off anywhere in it. Lucy's mum thought it would be nice to have something more stylish but knew that the practicality of the estate outweighed any argument in favour of something different being as it HAD been HER idea to get a dog two years previously and that it was great for transporting him around in the back!

Dad unlocked the car with his remote and got into the driver's seat. Lucy opened the back passenger door behind her dad and the little Nimnad jumped in. Then Lucy climbed in after him and sat down. As she started to buckle herself into her seatbelt her dad asked,

"What are you doing in the back Lucy? I feel like a cab driver."   Lucy thought for a moment and answered.

"Oh, erm, I thought it would make a change. Oh I mean... I don't know. I forgot........, I was thinking mum was getting in the front. Erm........, oh well never mind dad, I might as well stay here now." She stuttered, hoping her dad would leave it at that. Lucy wanted to hide her face and sit with her little friend but she couldn't tell her dad the real reason she was sitting in the back.

"Sometimes, Lucy, I wonder which planet you're living on," said dad. As he spoke to Lucy he turned the key in the ignition and pulled away from the house. Lucy and Nim looked at each other and giggled, that was the first time the Nimnad had experienced the feeling of laughter for himself.

"What are you giggling at?" Lucy's dad asked.

"Nothing dad," said Lucy, as she started laughing again. Lucy's dad gave in to her strange behaviour and continued on his way to Asda. On the way, Lucy noticed that she could see Nimnads here and there, randomly hanging around. Not that many, although she had never noticed them at all before the arrival of the little pink Nimnad, who, incidentally was leaping around the car, from the back to the front and back again! Plastering himself to the passenger door windows with great excitement, he'd never travelled in such an exciting way as in the motorcar!

"Sit down Nim." Lucy ordered.

"Pardon Lucy?" asked her dad.

"Oh, nothing," replied Lucy. "I didn't say anything." Lucy's dad could have sworn that he heard her say something. The Nimnad continued to leap around excitedly.

As dad pulled into the petrol garage there was a blue Nimnad standing by the newspaper rack.

"Look Nim, there's a blue one over there!" squealed Lucy.

"Now I know you said something that time Lucy," said her dad. Lucy thought quickly and replied. "Yes dad I did. I said don't forget mum wanted a newspaper, you might as well get it here."

"I don't remember mum asking for a newspaper," replied her dad looking at her a bit suspiciously.

"Well that's because she asked ME to ask you dad." Said Lucy, thinking quickly again.

"Oh, alright then," he said, and he got out of the car. He began to make his way across the forecourt to the shop as he temporarily forgot to put the petrol in the car, which was what he was there for in the first place! But due to Lucy's behaviour his brain was now turning to mush and he had got himself in a muddle. Lucy thought that if she could get her dad to walk through the blue Nimnad then he would get some good luck. Now, this was a bit crafty of Lucy really because luck is supposed to be unpredictable but she couldn't resist it! Just as her dad was about to reach the paper stand the little pink Nimnad spotted the blue one and began to wave frantically.

"Look that's my friend over there. I haven't seen him for years!" he said excitedly in a raised voice.
The Nimnads could go for a very long time between meeting up with each other due to the fact that they didn't usually have any control over when and where they might be.
Just as Lucy's dad approached the paper stand, the blue Nimnad suddenly spotted Nim waving from the car window. His face lit up and he began to walk towards the car. Lucy's stomach turned over. "Nooo!" she thought. "Dad's going to miss him!" She thought very quickly again, opened the window and shouted.

"Dad! you've forgotten to put the petrol in!"
He rolled his eyes, turned around and started back across the forecourt. As he was getting near to the car he collided with the blue Nimnad and walked straight through it. Nim couldn't believe it! Just as he was about to say hello to his long lost friend, 'Poof', he disappeared in a puff of blue smoke!

"Oh great, what the hell did you do that for?" Nim moaned as he looked at Lucy. But her plan had worked! Now all that remained was to wait and see what good luck her dad would receive. In all her excitement Lucy hadn't noticed how sad the little pink Nimnad was looking as he sat in the back of the car. Lucy's dad opened the petrol cap on the car, put the nozzle in and started to fill the tank. It was at that point that Lucy sat back in her seat breathing a sigh of relief. She turned to her friend with a smile to be greeted with a look of disappointment from him.

"What's the matter Nim?" she asked.

Just as he was about to reply, Lucy saw her dad walking towards the shop to pay for the petrol and the newspaper. To her horror she suddenly noticed a pink Nimnad standing by the entrance to the shop!

"Dad!!" she shouted out in desperation, hoping to distract him and knock him off course, but it was too late! He couldn't hear her and he walked straight through the pink one. Poof! A puff of pink smoke and it was gone! And so was dad's good luck! Both Lucy and Nim sat in silence in the back of the car and waited for dad to come back. Lucy was going to need a better plan next time if she was to succeed.

Lucy's dad arrived back at the car, having paid for the petrol, and the newspaper, and having had a close encounter with a blue Nimnad...... and a pink one! He got into the car and this time he didn't bother to ask Lucy to get into the front seat. He just started the car and drove out of the petrol garage.

By the time they had left, Lucy had buckled her seat belt back up and was gazing out of the window thinking of ways that she could make her dad get his good luck back again. About ten minutes later they arrived at the entrance to Asda. Lucy's dad pulled into the car park, found a space and parked the car.

"Right, come on then, let's get this spaghetti and get home," he said cheerfully. Lucy turned to the Nimnad and said, "come on then, let's go." And they all got out of the car. Her dad thought that she was answering him so he didn't question her talking to herself that time.

"Shall I get a trolley?" Lucy asked.

"We won't need one love," replied dad.

"Oh go on, just one of those small ones dad? it's easier than carrying stuff and you might see something else that we need." She pleaded.

What Lucy really meant was that SHE might see something else that SHE needs! She had a habit of putting all sorts of extras in the basket when she went shopping with her mum. Her dad frowned at her and passed her the trolley token that he kept attached to the car keys.

"Go on then, but hurry up," he said, and she went to fetch a trolley. They entered the shop and started to walk around. The little Nimnad was close on Lucy's tail, following her every move.

They hadn't been in the shop for more than a couple of minutes and were on their way to the pasta and rice aisle when Lucy spotted a blue Nimnad hovering around in the ready meals aisle!

"Oh, erm, dad, d'you know if mum brought any sausage rolls for my packed lunches?" asked Lucy, awkwardly.

"I have got no idea," he replied.

"Well I'm going to get some just in case." She said firmly and hurried off down the ready meals aisle to look for the sausage rolls, and the blue Nimnad of course! Nim was frantically running along behind Lucy and trying to keep up with her. "Wait a minute!" dad called out as he turned and started to follow in Lucy's direction. By now she was half way down the ready meals looking from left to right, and scanning the area ahead of her.

"He's gone, he's nowhere to be seen. How can that be?" Lucy thought. She hadn't seen anyone walk into him and anyway, if they had then she would have seen the puff of blue smoke?

"Have you got them?" Lucy's dad asked her.

"Got what? Lucy replied.

"The sausage rolls." Her dad answered, beginning to get irritated by her strange behaviour again.

"Oh!..... The sausage rolls?" she said with a look of bewilderment on her face. "No I can't see them. Come on dad I won't bother." She said, totally preoccupied with what she was really looking for. They continued down the ready meals aisle and back into the pasta and rice aisle. As they started to walk down the aisle Lucy spotted the blue Nimnad again!

"Come on dad, quick, let's get the spaghetti!" she said in a very loud, excited voice, and started to hurry down the aisle.

"Blimey Lucy what's the rush? one minute you're looking for extras and the next minute you're racing around the shop like there's no tomorrow!" remarked Lucy's dad in an equally loud voice, although he wasn't very excited. All the while the little Nimnad was following Lucy around like a shadow. He was beginning to feel a little disappointed with Lucy's behaviour, owing to the fact that she seemed to be more preoccupied with looking for the other Nimnads, rather than appreciating the fact that she had a Nimnad all of her very own. This was a very rare and special gift indeed. Unfortunately, the human nature of greed seemed to be overtaking Lucy's thoughts at that moment.

"Dad, you get the spaghetti and I'll look after the trolley," said Lucy. Her dad couldn't understand what the big deal was about her looking after the trolley and he gave her a look of utter confusion............AGAIN!

"Well, someone might steal it and it's got your trolley token in it dad." She said, trying to justify her actions and smiling sweetly at him.

"Oh, whatever you say love," he replied as he rolled his eyes at her and shook his head. He was getting quite fed up with all the messing around now.

The blue Nimnad was standing just in front of the rice, which was just before the spaghetti, and Lucy's dad would have to walk right through it to reach the spaghetti. She hoped and prayed that this time nothing would go wrong. But, Just as her dad got there the blue Nimnad turned and walked straight into the shelves! He had walked slowly towards the packets of rice and straight into them... And then... he'd disappeared! No puff of smoke or anything? He just walked right through! Just like you would imagine a ghost walking through a wall! Lucy ran off up the aisle and left the trolley where it was. The little pink Nimnad was running after her.

"Lucy! Come back! You need to calm down! What about me?" he shouted out after her. She didn't even hear him because she was so frantic about catching up with the blue Nimnad. She skidded round the end of the aisle and stared along the next one, which happened to be home baking by the way! There were a few people down that aisle. A mum with a toddler in a trolley, looking at cake mixes. An elderly lady looking at the jam and a middle aged man, who was standing in front of the flour. Lucy stood still for a moment, scanning the aisle for the Nimnad. Then dad appeared beside her looking quite annoyed.

"Look Lucy, I don't know what's going on with you tonight, but I've got the spaghetti AND the trolley and I'm going to pay and get out of here, come on." He said firmly. Just then, the blue Nimnad reappeared! He stepped out of the shelves as if by magic! It was as though he had walked into the shelf down the other aisle, straight through, and back out of it in this one? Lucy couldn't believe it.

"Alright dad, come on then." she complied, and she started to run down the aisle. Just as she reached the middle-aged man, she looked back to check that her dad was following, and as she did so, she bumped into the man knocking him sideways. The man stumbled and grabbed onto Lucy's arm to stop himself from falling over but the little pink Nimnad was getting caught up in the middle of them and... "Uh oh!" thought the Nimnad. POOF! Puff of pink smoke and he was gone! The man's leg had passed right through him! Lucy looked down and saw the pink smoke, but she didn't seem bothered.

"Oops sorry." She said to the man and steadied him back on to his feet again. She could still see the blue Nimnad further down the aisle. With Nim gone for now, it was just Lucy and her dad.

"Come on then dad, hurry up. Let's get home," she said as though she were the parent!

"Be careful Lucy, that's enough of this silly behaviour. I've had enough..........I don't know what's come over you tonight?" he said angrily.

"Sorry dad." She said, very insincerely.
Suddenly the blue Nimnad crossed the aisle and disappeared into the shelves again!

"I don't believe it!" Lucy thought, getting angry now. Just then, she and her dad heard a man's voice let out a loud "ARGH!!!" They both looked around to see what had happened. It was the middle-aged man! He had picked up a bag of self-raising flour from the shelf and it must have burst!

A cloud of white dust surrounded the man and he had a thin layer of white flour lying on his eyelashes. It was in his hair and all down the front of his clothes!

"Poor man." The mum said to her little boy.

"What bad luck." The old lady said to him. She had been looking at the jam but was now brushing the flour off the man's clothes whilst trying to make him feel slightly less embarrassed. Lucy wanted to laugh but thought it best not to, given the mood that her dad was now in and anyway, she was still intent on finding the blue Nimnad! Lucy's dad insisted they walk straight from that aisle to the next and down towards the check out. She thought she'd better not argue with him.... For now anyway.

They started to walk down the washing powder and liquids aisle, towards the check out and Lucy's tummy started to churn. You know that feeling you get when temptation overcomes you and you just can't resist something? Well that's what happened to Lucy. She had a tingling in her fingers and toes and her face became hot and flushed. All she could think about was the blue Nimnad. She couldn't leave the supermarket without getting her dad to walk through it! She couldn't resist the temptation any longer. When they reached the end of the aisle she did a sharp left turn and started to run back up the next aisle. To her surprise, her little pink Nimnad appeared beside her!

"Lucy what's been going on?" he asked.

"Lucy! Come back here now!" her dad shouted. He was really angry now.

"I just remembered something important dad, follow me quick." She said, turning her head towards her dad and beckoning him in the direction that she was running. Sensing the urgency in her voice he followed her in a hurry, thinking that this must be something very important.

"Come on dad. Quick!" Lucy called out again. Her dad was now picking up speed behind her and the little pink Nimnad as they ran along in front of him. Lucy could see the blue Nimnad in the distance. It was hovering around in the aisle up ahead of them. She was desperate to reach it with her dad before it disappeared again. All inhibitions were gone from Lucy and she was oblivious to anything and anyone around her now. All she cared about was catching up with the blue Nimnad. So much was her panic to catch it that she tripped over a shop assistant who was kneeling on the floor unpacking some boxes of chocolates that he had been carefully building into a very artistic display. Lucy landed flat out on her tummy and slid along the floor as if she was on ice! The shop assistant fell forwards, knocking into his display, which tumbled to the floor like an avalanche! There were boxes of chocolates everywhere! Lucy's dad sped up, clambering over the chocolates to get to his daughter to make sure that she wasn't hurt. In all of this pandemonium Lucy had actually caught up with, and slid past the blue Nimnad, who at that moment was still hovering in the aisle, oblivious to what was going on! Her dad was in such a hurry to get to her that he barged past a woman who was watching in amazement, at the antics that were going on. As he knocked her off balance she called out, "EXCUSE ME!!! Do you mind looking where you are going?"

Lucy's dad turned to apologise as the woman stormed towards him looking as though she was going to give him a piece of her mind. Lucy laid on the floor watching and realised that there was nothing else she could do now..... The woman had beaten her dad to it. She'd walked right through the blue Nimnad. 'POOF!, a puff of blue smoke and he was gone.

"Look, I'm really very sorry," said Lucy's dad. "But at the moment I'm very concerned about my daughter. I don't think she's feeling very well."
He then walked away from the woman and towards Lucy, who by now was picking herself up from the floor and brushing herself down. The little pink Nimnad was staring at Lucy with a very sad look on his face...... again!

"Come on Lucy, let's get you home before you cause some real damage." Said her dad. "I'll think twice before I ask you to come shopping with me again." He said with a stern expression on his face.
Lucy wasn't sure whether her dad was joking with her or if he was really angry. They stood in silence at the checkout as he paid for the spaghetti and then they left the supermarket.
As they walked out and past the escalator that led to the upper car park, Lucy heard raised voices.

"Look dad." She said sheepishly, pointing at the escalator. It was the woman who had walked into the blue Nimnad. She had been holding her shopping in carrier bags and the handles must have broken. There were tins of peas and baked beans rolling down the escalator and people were trying to dodge or jump over them as they rolled down. The woman was trying to salvage her shopping, tucking things under her arms whilst concentrating on trying not to fall over!

"It must have been the blue Nimnad?" Lucy thought. She offered to put the trolley back whilst dad walked to the car. The little pink Nimnad quietly followed Lucy around. Not another word was exchanged between them for a while. When Lucy reached the car she found her dad standing beside it, cursing and moaning.

"What's wrong dad?" Lucy asked.

"I don't believe it! I've got a flat tyre now!" he said with a raised and angry voice. He took a deep breath and continued.

"I must have driven over a nail or something! Oh it's no good, I'll have to put the spare on. I can't drive home with it like that."

"What now?" groaned Lucy.

"Yes NOW." He replied sharply.

It was a chilly evening and was beginning to drizzle with rain.

"You go back inside and look at the magazines or something, and I'll come and get you when I've finished it."

"Ok dad." She said, feeling a mixture of emotions ranging from disappointment and tiredness, to guilt. She felt sorry for her dad because of the grief that she had put him through in the supermarket, but she still felt a desperate need to find him some good luck. A tired, fed up Lucy and a very deflated Nimnad plodded back across the car park towards the escalator. As they reached the entrance, two large glass doors automatically parted and slid open to allow them to walk in. The warmth of the hot air inside the store hit Lucy and made her feel all warm and cosy. She made her way across the foyer towards the magazines, followed by Nim. As she picked up a magazine, she turned to the little Nimnad and asked him,

"Nim, just what are you able to do? I mean what was going on back there in the shop?" she paused and thought for a moment.

"How come that Blue Nimnad kept disappearing down one aisle and then reappearing in the next?" she paused again. "No one walked through it, did they? I don't understand." She finished her interrogation with a puzzled look on her face.

"Don't be silly Lucy," he replied. "It's quite simple really. You can't touch us without us disappearing, but we can pass through anything that's in our pathway and nothing happens. Good isn't it?"

"What do you mean? Can you walk through walls?" Lucy asked.

"Yes, that's exactly what I mean," chuckled the Nimnad, happy that he had gained Lucy's attention for the first time since they had left the house. She let out a big sigh, as she gazed at the magazine she was holding. She opened it and began to browse over the pages. Not content to be dispensed with so quickly, Nim decided to play a trick on Lucy. All of a sudden, his face came out of the middle of the page, looked straight at Lucy and winked! She looked down beside her to where he had been just a moment ago but he was gone. She looked back at the page again and said, "What the hell are you doing in there?"

"It's like I said Lucy," he smiled. "I can go anywhere I want to." Then he chuckled and disappeared from the page. Lucy noticed that there was a gentleman just along from where she was standing and he was giving her a very funny look. She thought quickly and began to read aloud. She realised that the man must have thought that she was talking to herself! Of course, under normal circumstances the little pink Nimnad wouldn't have been able to play around like he was, but then, these weren't normal circumstances for him, were they? The man raised his eyebrows as he looked Lucy up and down and wandered off to the counter to pay for his newspaper and Lucy looked for the Nimnad.

"Lucy! Look! Here I am!" She heard a voice call out from somewhere on the shelves where she was now standing in front of a display of DVD's. Instinctively she looked down and there he was again!
His little pink face was protruding through one of the DVD cases!

"How did you get in there?" she asked, puzzled.

"Oh, you know.....it's just one of my many talents." He said, in a very sure of himself way.

"Pardon dear?" a lady said who was standing beside Lucy.

"Sorry?" Lucy said as she frowned.

"Are you ok dear?" asked the lady. "I thought you said something, are you alright dear?"

"Yes....., yes thank you," answered Lucy. "I was just thinking aloud that's all."

"Oh alright dear." The lady smiled and walked away. The little pink Nimnad's face was still smiling at Lucy from within the case of the DVD! She picked it up and walked back over to the magazines, talking to it as she went. Well at least that's what it looked like to people in the store!

"Get out of there now." Lucy demanded in a cross voice. "This isn't funny anymore." With that, Nim shot out of the case as if fired out of a cannon! Straight through a floral display in the middle of the foyer and landed on top of a mechanical train ride, which for fifty pence small children could sit on as it glided backwards and forwards making 'choo choo' noises as it moved.

Lucy burst out laughing, Nim looked so funny. He had rose petals on his head and was dancing around on the roof of the train making funny faces at her. She was splitting her sides with laughter as she rushed over to the train. By now quite a few people had noticed Lucy's strange behaviour (again!) Even the security guard had moved in a little closer to keep an eye on her. He was puzzled as to why there were rose petals floating around on the roof of the train!

"Oh Nim! You're so funny! You've really cheered me up....., thanks." She said sincerely.

"Just doing my job." He replied, winking at Lucy with a smile on his face. Just then, dad appeared in the entrance to the store and he was looking around for Lucy.

"Over here dad!" she called out, waving her hand in the air so that he would notice her. He walked over to where she was standing.

"What are you doing playing around with this? aren't you a bit too old?" he was looking at the train.

"Yeah I am. I was just getting a bit bored that's all." She answered.

"Right then," he said. "I'm just going to use the loo and clean my hands up. Can you call mum and let her know what happened, and tell her we'll be on our way home soon?"

"Ok dad." Said Lucy, as she took out her mobile to call her mum.

Nim had now stopped playing around and waited patiently with Lucy for her dad to return.

After what seemed like no time at all he was back.

"Let's get home and have some dinner, I'm starving."

"Me too." Lucy replied. She felt relieved that dad didn't seem to be so angry with her anymore. Nim sat on the rear seat of the car looking exhausted. This was the first time he had ever experienced the feeling of tiredness and it was as much as he could do to keep his eyes open. Lucy looked round at him and smiled.

Back home mum was eagerly waiting for the spaghetti and Ryan was starting to moan because he was hungry. There was the sound of keys in the front door and in came dad, Lucy and of course the Nimnad, who incidentally seemed to have replenished his energy levels already. He wandered off around the house on his own to get himself acquainted with the nooks and crannies, making sure to avoid Buddy at all times for fear that it would bring on an attack of the sneezes... The Nimnad didn't like sneezing very much.

The family sat down to a great big plate of spaghetti bolognaise each. Mum always put far too much dinner on everybody's plate, but they were all used to that so nobody said anything about it.

After dinner it was a very quiet evening, which quite frankly Lucy didn't object to at all as she could do with a break from all of the excitement. By eleven thirty the lights were out and everyone was in bed.

"Goodnight Nim," whispered Lucy.

"Is it?"

"No, "giggled Lucy. "That's not what I mean. It's what we say to each other when we are going to bed and we won't speak to each other until the next day." She explained.

"Oh, I see." Nim had a little giggle too.

"Goodnight Lucy."

"Goodnight..., again." She whispered, and that was that until morning

APRONS AND OVEN GLOVES

The next day was Friday, which apart from Saturday and Sunday was Lucy's favourite day of the week because it was the last day of school before the weekend. She crawled out of bed to the usual sound of her own voice coming from her phone. She dragged herself to the bathroom with her eyes practically shut, aimed the toothpaste at her toothbrush and took a lucky shot. Lucy brushed her teeth and got washed with the same sinking feeling in her stomach that she had every school day. It was the 'I don't want to go to school' feeling. She couldn't put the feeling into a rational, understandable description for anyone who hadn't been bullied to be able to understand, but it was very real for her. It was a feeling that she would do anything to get rid of, but she couldn't shake it off. Anyway, as soon as she was ready and she had eaten about three bites of toast, taken a sip of tea, and kissed mum goodbye, she was off out of the front door and on her way to school. For some kids, school is an enjoyable experience. Something to look forward to. For some kids, school is a very important part of their life and something that they find very fulfilling and rewarding. Some even find school fun! but not Lucy. For her, it was just a recurring nightmare that she relived every day for five days of the week, every week (except for the holidays, which she was on a permanent countdown to... Oh, and the days when she managed to hide in her bedroom!) It was such a shame that something so positive had become something to be so feared.... But it had.

Lucy looked down at the cute little creature that had entered her life and wondered how on earth it was going to make such a big difference to the things that were REALLY causing her so much stress. She couldn't imagine ever being free from the knots in her stomach, the ache in her limbs and the horrible feeling of worthlessness that so often ran through her body. Thankfully, she arrived at School undetected by the bullies for a change and she managed to make it to her form room for registration without any problems. Mr Watson was sitting at his desk looking at the register.

"Quiet girls, listen for your name please!" he shouted above a drone of voices chatting to each other in the classroom. He called the register and then everyone dispersed into the general direction of their first lesson. Lucy's first lesson was food tech, and for today's lesson they were going to be making meringues. In case you don't already know, meringues are not at all easy to make. You've either got the knack or you haven't! The trick is, to get lots of air into an egg white whilst whisking it in a bowl and hopefully when you bake it, having added some sugar etc, it comes out of the oven as a beautiful crunchy meringue. To look at, it should resemble something like a white fluffy cloud with little mountain peaks on the top of it that are a light golden colour, not too dark but just lightly crisp. Well, Lucy wasn't much looking forward to this lesson as Miss Price, her 'food tech' teacher was very prim and proper and quite strict too.

Lucy entered the Kitchen where the lesson was to be held and sat down at her table which she shared with another girl called Olivia. Olivia was a quiet, unassuming girl who was very studious and kept herself to herself. In other words, quite boring as a partner in the Kitchen. Miss Price entered the Kitchen and all the girls faced the front and looked at her. Although she wasn't exactly scary, she carried an air of authority with her that seemed to command respect from the girls. She was tall and slim, with auburn hair, which she always wore tied back in a French Platt and always dressed with care in a very lady like fashion. She never wore trousers, always a skirt or a dress. At this point the little Nimnad was standing beside Lucy watching what was going on. He was looking around the Kitchen, checking to see if there was any of the Mackenzie lot in there. Over in the far corner he could see Beth busily arranging her ingredients in front of her. Cooking happened to be her favourite subject at School and it was the one thing that she excelled in, so she wouldn't be best pleased if someone in the class did better than her!

"Right then ladies, shall we begin?" asked Miss Price, although she wasn't really asking them, she was actually telling them in a polite manner that they were going to begin.

"Start by cracking your eggs and separating the yolk from the white. You need only the white of the egg to make your meringue." And so they all began.

The sound of cracking eggshells filled the Kitchen. There wasn't any chatting going on because the girls were too busy concentrating on what they were doing. Next they put some sugar into their mixing bowls and then Miss Price told them all to plug in their electric whisks.

"Ok ladies, you need to whisk your mixture until it is light and fluffy, white in colour, and you can form little peaks on the top like little mountain tops." Said Miss Price, as she paced around the room briefly observing everyone.

All of the girls stood to attention by their tables as if awaiting room inspection! Then as if by synchronisation the whisking began. The Nimnad was still carefully looking around the Kitchen keeping a check on everyone's progress. Some faces looked very calm and relaxed. Others were not so relaxed, and when he looked at Lucy's face she looked absolutely gutted.

"What is it Lucy?" he asked. "What's wrong?"

"My meringue won't froth up." She answered.

"No talking Lucy Miles." Said Miss Price in a firm voice. "Girls, I just need to leave you on your own for five minutes. I will be back before you know it." She said.

These were the words Lucy always dreaded hearing because she knew what that meant for her. As soon as Miss Price had left the classroom it started. In synchronisation several of the girls led by Beth started calling out.

"Bitch, Bitch! Bitch! Bitch! BITCH!" Then screwed up bits of paper started hitting Lucy on the back of the head. This went on for several minutes. Lucy knew this would continue until Miss Price returned, as it was the same in every class whenever a teacher left the room. It had been going on for so long that Lucy had become numb to it. It did bother her a lot, but for her, it was a normal part of school life. Her eyes widened in the direction of the Nimnad as she tried to talk to him through eye contact. No words were needed. The little pink Nimnad could see what she wanted and he knew what he had to do.

Lucy was beginning to give up hope of ever getting her meringue mixture to look anything like a molehill let alone the peak of a mountain! She reached behind herself and felt for her stool to sit on. As she dragged it in behind her, the Nimnad seized his opportunity and climbed up onto the stool and as Lucy sat down she sat straight on him too! He closed his eyes and waited to disappear! Lucy rested her body on the stool and sighed as she felt completely defeated. As she sat there feeling sorry for herself she became aware of the fact that she was being engulfed with pink smoke! She began to smile because she instantly realised what had happened. She quickly stood up and started to whisk her meringue mixture again. She was trying frantically to make it look like a mountain! As she continued to whisk she noticed that the mixture was beginning to feel firmer. She switched the whisk off and laid it down on the table and with a wide-eyed look of hope on her face she gently tapped the top of the mixture with the back of a spoon, and THEY were there! Lucy had mountaintops, peaks, whatever they were called she had them! Just at that moment Miss Price arrived beside Lucy's table! She peered into the bowl.

"Yes indeed Lucy that is definitely ready to bake. Quickly gather round everyone! I want to show you what a perfect meringue mixture should look like! Quickly class before it sinks!" she called out in her firm but ladylike fashion. All the girls came to see the celebrated meringues. A few of the girls congratulated Lucy by saying, "well done." Some said nothing and others were clearly jealous, especially Beth Mackenzie, who simply leaned forward and whispered into Lucy's ear.

"You're in for it at lunch."

The excitement that Lucy had felt about being the best meringue maker of the day was gone in an instant. Instead, all she could feel was the knot in her stomach, the tingling in her legs and the tremble of her arms. Her body ached with fear. That feeling had become normal.

Lucy quietly packed her things away at the end of the lesson, including her prize baked meringues, which she had carefully placed into a container with a tightly fitting lid so that they wouldn't get broken. She was hoping to make it home from school with them intact so that she could take pride in showing them to her mum.

At the sound of the lunchtime bell the class was dismissed by Miss Price and everyone left the kitchen in a fairly orderly fashion. As Lucy approached the door to exit the kitchen she was met with a glare from Beth. Lucy just looked down at the floor and carried on walking. She wasn't very keen on lunchtimes. I mean she liked lunchtime because she was always hungry and looked forward to eating her lunch, but on the other hand, she didn't like it much because she didn't really have a best friend to hang around with. There were groups of girls that she could stand with, but nobody in particular who she felt she belonged with. This alone used to make Lucy feel very lonely when the bullies would start picking on her because she didn't feel that she had anybody who she could turn to for support who would care enough to stick up for her as you would do for a best friend if somebody was upsetting them. Sometimes Lucy would take herself off to a quiet step around the back of the canteen and sit alone eating her lunch. It seemed a better option than running the risk of bumping into the Mackenzie mob, and today that's what she chose to do.

"Come on Nim." She said. "Let's sit here."

"Don't worry Lucy, you're not on your own. Don't forget you've got me now." Nim tried to reassure her.
Lucy took comfort in that, and didn't feel quite so alone as usual. She smiled at him and then unwrapped her sandwiches.

She was minding her own business when Beth and her lot appeared around the corner....., all of them! She could feel their presence as they walked towards her. She felt very intimidated. A desperate need to get up and run swept over her, but she knew that she couldn't. She felt trapped as the usual knots and trembling swept over her. They had seen her, and they knew that she had seen them too! There was no way out..... Beth was coming to confront her and there was nothing Lucy could do about it.

As they came closer they spread out like a fan in front of the step where Lucy was sitting, she could hardly catch her breath as she waited to find out what was going to happen next. They stood there towering over her, looking down at her. They looked mean and spiteful, looking her up and down with their hands on their hips. The piece of sandwich that she'd just bitten off nearly stuck in her throat.

"I think you've got something of mine, bitch." Said Beth.

"I don't think so?" Lucy gulped as she swallowed the piece of sandwich whole, almost choking on it.

"Don't mess with me, you idiot." Beth bit at Lucy. "You've got my meringues and I want 'em now!"

"No I haven't." Lucy's voice quivered as she tried to cough her words out.

Well what's in that white container next to you then?" Beth asked as she pointed at the plastic container that had Lucy's meringues in.

"Er, um, they're my meringues." Lucy tried to stick up for herself.

"I don't think so you stupid bitch. They're mine! Ain't they girls?" asked Beth, looking round at her 'friends' for a reaction.

"Yeah, course they are." Carley nodded her head and raised her eyebrows, as she laughed at Beth's meanness.

"I saw you make them myself." Chuckled Amber as she looked around to check that no-one was coming.

Lucy could feel a lack of control sweep over her as Beth started to come towards her. She put her hand on top of the container to protect it, but Beth just laughed and so did the rest of the mob. Nim felt a duty to protect Lucy, and anything that mattered to her and so he quietly spoke into her ear.

"It's alright, you can let go. It'll be ok."

"Are you sure?" Lucy asked, as she turned to look at him.

"Hey listen, she's talking to herself now!" Kerry shouted to the others.

"She's more stupid than I thought!" Beth laughed as she lunged towards Lucy, shoving her as she grabbed the container.

"Talking to meringues now are you? You're so weird." Beth said sarcastically, as she ran away, followed by the rest of the girls. Lucy started to cry.

"Oh Lucy, I'm so sorry. Please don't cry." Nim Said. "I promise I'll get your meringues back to you before the end of the day. Don't worry, we'll show them what we're made of."

Lucy spent the afternoon playing hockey and netball, neither of which she particularly liked. Trying to play hockey on a muddy, rain soaked field, she liked even less! But I suppose anything was better than being stuck in a classroom with people she didn't like! At the end of PE all the girls went to have a shower and get ready to go home. Luckily none of Lucy's enemies were in the PE group. She met up with Nim at her space on the bench in the changing rooms, where he had been sitting, trying to think of ways to get the meringues back.

"Hello Nim." Lucy said as she put her shoes and coat on.

"Hello. Are you alright?" he asked her.

"Yep, I just can't wait to get home now, I hate it here."

"Come on Lucy, let's get out of here." He said.

They left the changing room and the hustle and bustle that filled the steamy air inside it. From there they walked along the corridor towards the double glass doors that led out into the playground. Once outside, they had to walk across the playground towards a gate that would let them out onto the pavement and they could start to make their way home. Lucy got halfway across the playground and she noticed a group of boys hanging around outside the gate near a bus stop. She could see in the distance that one of them was a boy called James Parkin. Beth fancied the pants off of him and Lucy hoped and prayed that he wasn't waiting there to meet Beth from school! Otherwise their paths might cross again a little sooner than Lucy felt she could handle!

"Look who it is!" a familiar voice shouted from behind Lucy. Lucy felt like she was going to throw up. She'd had just about as much of Beth and her lot as she could stomach for one day. She didn't dare look round, but judging by the hairs that she could feel standing up on the back of her neck and the grins on the boy's faces at the gate, she knew who was calling out.... AND she knew it was aimed at her.

"Want some nice meringues boys?" Beth called out.

"I made them myself, didn't I Lucy?" she said, trying to intimidate her, (and it was working).

Lucy put her head down and continued to walk in the direction of the gate. There wasn't anyone around as this wasn't an official exit from school and wasn't generally used by many of the girls or teachers. Beth was carrying Lucy's white container out in front of herself like a prize.

"Hey." Nim said. "Look over there Lucy".

Lucy didn't say a word but just looked where the Nimnad

was looking. Hovering around by the gate was a blue Nimnad. Now Nim knew that he wasn't supposed to interfere with the natural course of events so far as other Nimnads were concerned. However, even HE was prepared to make an exception on this occasion. Could it be that his judgement was being clouded by the human emotions he was becoming familiar with?

He started waving and jumping up and down frantically, trying to attract the attention of the blue Nimnad. As he was making such a commotion there were pink sparks flying from his hair! Lucy could see them and it was apparently obvious that the blue Nimnad could see them too as he was clearly attracted to them because he was moving in their direction. Lucy wasn't quite sure what her little friend was doing but she was too scared to ask for fear of being laughed at by the others so she just continued to walk straight ahead. Nim had guessed that Beth would make a move soon, and he'd guessed right! She started to pick up speed and ran past Lucy, shoving her in the arm as she went. She was laughing and had a really mean look on her face. It was quite obvious that she intended to give Lucy's meringues to James Parkin. The blue Nimnad was still slowly making its way across the playground, and oblivious to its existence, Beth ran straight through it! With a puff of blue smoke it disappeared! The damage was done.

"Yes! Yes! It worked!" The little Nimnad shouted, jumping up and down with excitement. Within seconds, Beth tripped and fell flat on her face! Her legs and arms sprawled out like a starfish! Lucy's container flew out of Beth's hands and slid across the ground. The little pink Nimnad could see what was coming next so he ran towards the container and leapt on top of it, clinging to the lid with his little arms and legs. James Parkin stepped inside the gate and picked the container up, putting his hand straight through him! 'POOF!' A puff of pink smoke and he was gone! Only this time he appeared straight back at Lucy's side. He was becoming crafty. James Parkin turned to make a run for it up the road, swiftly followed by his mates, when the door of a parked car opened, stopping James in his tracks. On closer inspection it was his mum in her new Mercedes sports car!

"What are you doing here James?" she asked. "Jump in and I'll give you a lift home." She said.
Totally in awe of his mum's fancy new sports car he dumped his mates and the meringues and jumped in. He put on his seat belt and took a can of coke from his blazer pocket. As he opened it, the coke exploded in a shower of fizz all over him and the dashboard of his mum's new car! There was sticky coke everywhere! His friends who had been watching and admiring the new car began to laugh their heads off, pointing and calling out. "Nice one James!"

"You stupid boy that's the last time you're getting in this car!" shouted his mum. "And you can clean it all up as soon as we get home too!" she snapped in a loud, angry voice. As she sped off down the road his mates wandered off laughing and chatting to each other. Lucy, accompanied by Nim walked quietly over to the curb where her container was sitting, picked it up and made her way home.

STRIKE!

That evening, over dinner (which was a chip butty, chocolate milkshake and a bowl of Lucy and Ryan's favourite mint choc chip ice cream, owing to the fact that her parents had gone next door into the neighbour's house for a curry and a few drinks). Lucy decided to tell her brother about the Nimnad.

As Lucy sat at the kitchen table she tried to muster up the courage to tell Ryan about her new friend, but each time she drew a breath to speak, she got butterflies in her stomach and the words wouldn't come out. She was afraid that Ryan wouldn't believe her and then she would feel stupid. Ryan was always telling stories that weren't true, stringing people along just for a laugh and then telling them that he was only joking, so Lucy was thinking that he might think that she was just trying to play him at his own game.

"Are you alright Lucy?" Ryan asked.

Staring into her ice cream, which was now more like a bowl of whipped cream from where Lucy had stirred it around so much, she replied, "Yeah, I'm fine. It's just that....." Lucy tapered off and paused, still staring into her ice cream.

"What?" Ryan asked curiously.

Lucy's eyes, until then still firmly fixed on her ice cream, shifted upwards and onto Ryan's face. She stared at him for a moment.

"It's just that there's something I really want to tell you, but I don't think you're gonna believe me."

"Well tell me what it is then, and I'll tell you if I believe you or not."

"See? that's what I mean. If I tell you.....," Lucy paused again and let out a big sigh.

"I need to know that you will DEFINITELY believe me, 'cause I'm scared that if you don't then you might go and tell someone else. I can't have that. It's the biggest secret I've ever had to keep and I can't believe it's happening to me."

"Well ok then what IS it Luce?" Ryan was getting impatient.

"You have to promise not to tell ANYONE." She was looking him straight in the eyes. "I mean it Ryan. Not mum, not dad, NO-ONE."

"OK OK! for god's sake Lucy!..... I get the message." He quietened his voice back down.

"Just tell me what it IS. I believe you already and you haven't even told me what it IS yet." He sat back in his chair looking a bit fed up now.

"Ok. Well...., I was fast asleep in bed on Thursday night when Buddy started barking in my room and woke me up. He was running round my bedroom, jumping around like a maniac." She paused for a moment to think......

"Anyway, I told him to be quiet and was trying to go back to sleep when he started again. You're not gonna believe this Ryan............" She took a deep breath. "In the middle of my cuddlies was this weird little creature. Honestly Ryan, I've never seen anything like it before. You won't believe your eyes when you see it." She said to him with a convincing look on her face.

"Well what IS it then?"Ryan was becoming very interested now.

The whole time Lucy had been having this conversation with Ryan, Nim had been sitting on the floor in the corner of the kitchen listening to them. He felt very sad and disappointed in Lucy. He thought that he meant more to her. He couldn't believe that she was telling Ryan about him. After everything that Nim had explained to her about good and bad luck, pink and blue Nimnads, the level of trust that he had put in Lucy, the biggest secret that he could have shared with a human.... HIS special human. He thought she realised how precious their friendship was, and now she was going to expose him to another human. Albeit this other human was Lucy's brother, a member of her family, that wasn't the point. Lucy had betrayed the little pink Nimnads trust.

"Well," said Lucy. "It's called a Nimnad...., and it's been sent to me to bring me some good luck because I've been having such at a tough time with Beth and her mates." She studied Ryan's face to see if he believed what she was saying.

"Apparently, Nimnads are responsible for balancing how much luck each of us gets? sometimes it's good, sometimes it's bad. Whatever we get, they're the ones that give it to us."

"Apparently?..." Nim said to himself. He was really offended now.

"Yeah right." Ryan was grinning at Lucy. "Show me it and I'll believe you." he said sarcastically.

"IT!" Thought Nim. He was an 'IT' now?

"OK then. I will......... Buddy!" she shouted, "come on Buddy, come here!" Lucy called Buddy into the kitchen. He was looking a bit nervous as he walked slowly into the kitchen with his head hung low and his tail between his legs. He didn't really like to get so close to the Nimnad.

"ACHOO!" went the Nimnad.

"Yay! it worked." Said Lucy, looking very smug. "There," she pointed. "Over there in the corner. Look, can you see him?"

Ryan stared into the corner of the room.

"What IS that thing?" He asked.

The poor little Nimnad sneezed again.

"That's him!" Lucy could hardly contain herself. "That's MY Nimnad. Isn't he cute?"

"Oh yeah, he's brilliant. That's amazing Lucy, can you keep him forever?" Ryan asked convincingly.

"I'm not sure?" she said, looking very serious.

"OK, VERY FUNNY! You've got your own back on me. NIMNADS...., yeah right! And I believe in Father Christmas too." Ryan said, raising his eyebrows at Lucy.

"Can't you see him Ryan?"

"Of course I can't see him, there's nothing there to see stupid. You're SO funny Luce." He said. "I'm going to watch a film." And he stormed off.

The little Nimnad's eyes were burning into Lucy's with a massive look of disappointment. Surely she would realise from that look how desperately upset she had made him feel? But she didn't. Nim walked slowly out of the kitchen and made his way up to Lucy's bedroom. Leaving Lucy to plot and scheme how she could have some fun with him over the weekend. It was about 11pm when mum and dad came home and Lucy had gone to bed exhausted, with a mind full of plans for the next day.

Uncle Ray and auntie Sue were coming to stay for the weekend, bringing Lucy and Ryan's cousins, Leanne, Christopher and Jason with them. Uncle Ray was Lucy's dad's brother. Her dad and her uncle didn't always get on that well together. There had always been an element of competition between them when they were growing up and that element had never gone away, but they never gave up trying to get along with each other for the sake of the rest of the family....., and a little bit for themselves as well.

Lucy slept very deeply that night and it was 9.50am when she woke up. Ryan's head was poking through the small gap where her door was open, as though levitating on its own.

"Come on Lucy, you getting up?" he inquired. "They'll be here soon."

"Who?" asked Lucy

"Leanne, Christopher and Jason!" Ryan shouted, in an irritated voice because he couldn't believe that his sister had forgotten that they were coming for the weekend. Lucy flung her duvet back towards the wall and leapt out of bed. She had slept very well for a change and had woken in such a relaxed state that she had forgotten all about the weekend arrangements.

"Oh RYAN! You could have called me a bit earlier!" she called out as she opened her wardrobe, which had an array of clothes, shoes and belts, some on hangers and some just thrown at the shelves in the hopes that they would have a safe landing.

She stood and gazed into her organised mess as she did on a regular basis, trying to decide what to wear. Although how she could possibly see what was in there is anybody's guess. She delved in and came out with a pink hooded sweatshirt and a nice pair of light blue jeans. Forty minutes later, she had been in the shower, washed her hair, dried it and put it up into a ponytail with a white ribbon, and even managed to close her wardrobe doors!

There was a ring at the doorbell and Lucy jumped off her bed to look out of her window. She was excited because she was looking forward to spending time with her cousins and pleased because she knew that her mum and her auntie got along really well, and always enjoyed each other's company when they got the chance. But then there was always this little bit of anxiety that crept in because of the love/hate relationship that existed between her dad and her uncle. It was always a bit of a lottery as to whether they would get through a visit or social event without falling out with each other. But when they did get along, it was always great!

Lucy ran down the stairs to greet everyone in the hall as they arrived. Hugs and kisses were exchanged between everyone and they all made their way into the kitchen for a cuppa and a chat.

"Is it alright if I make some toast mum?" Lucy asked.

"Of course you can love," answered her mum. "Does anyone else want some?" nobody wanted toast as they'd eaten breakfast before they left home, which was only about two hours ago. All the same, Lucy's mum put a plate of biscuits out on the kitchen table just in case anybody wanted one with their cup of tea. When the tea had been made and some polite conversation had been exchanged, the family separated into different directions. Lucy quickly ate her toast and disappeared upstairs to compare games and gossip with Ryan and her cousins. Dad and uncle Ray went to sit in the lounge and discuss what to do for the evening, and mum and auntie Sue stayed in the kitchen so that they could talk about them all!

A bit later on, dad and uncle Ray suggested to mum and auntie Sue that they all go bowling for the evening, which they thought was a great idea. Lucy's dad phoned Tenpin bowling and booked the lanes.

A very pleasant day of chilling out and chatting passed, and at about 6.00pm they left the house in two cars for the short drive to the bowling alley, stopping at Burger King for dinner on the way.

Nim had remained quiet all day, following Lucy around like a shadow. No conversation had passed between them and he was beginning to feel as though Lucy was taking him for granted and that he was just there for her as and when she decided to 'use' him. That wasn't meant to be the arrangement and something was beginning to feel very wrong to the little Nimnad. He had been so happy until last night, but something had changed, and that something was Lucy's attitude.

The two families filled their bellies up with burgers and chips at Burger King and then left for an action packed evening of bowling and bedlam. Once they had arrived at Tenpin bowling, parked their cars and paid their lane fees it was time to get their bowling shoes on. One at a time they swapped their own shoes for a pair of hideous red and white lace up shoes specially designed for comfort and with a non slip sole. Although no one liked the look of them, no one could deny how comfy they were! Lucy's dad and uncle went to the bar to buy some drinks for everyone and her mum and auntie Sue guided the rest of them to the lanes that had been booked for them. There was one lane booked for the adults and one booked for the kids, right next door to each other.

They had arrived a bit too early and the lanes were still in use so the boys went for a wander over to the pool tables for a quick game whilst they were waiting. The girls however, didn't fancy pool so they made their way over to have a go on the dance mat (which Lucy was actually very good at.) About twenty-five minutes must have passed and auntie Sue went to round them all up to start bowling as the lanes were now free. All the kids wandered over laughing and chatting with each other. They were having a really good time, except that when they arrived at their lane Lucy was devastated to see that Beth and Amber were bowling on the lane next door but one!...... With two really fit boys from Ryan's school!

"Oh no!" She thought, her tummy turning over. "How embarrassing!...., I'll never live this down." She thought. Bowling was not Lucy's strongest talent. In fact, she was not very good at it at all, but she did enjoy it. So the fact that she wasn't very good at it didn't normally bother her. But tonight it did!

"What's wrong?" Nim asked her, looking very concerned.

"Look over there Nim." She pointed in the direction of

where Beth and Amber were standing with the boys. "It's Beth and Amber from my school with some boys from Ryan's. When they see how rubbish my bowling is they'll tell everyone at school, and they'll all have a good laugh at me." She frowned.

"Can't you go back to where you were before? You were really good at jumping around on that thing Lucy." He said.

"No I can't, and that THING is called a dance mat." She was agitated and snapped at Nim.

The family took their turns at bowling and when it came to Lucy, the bowling ball went straight into the gutter every time. Beth and Amber were watching from their lane and sniggering to each other. Lucy could sense them watching her but she didn't want to make a fuss and say anything to her mum and dad.

"Nim.... You've got to give me some good luck." She said to the little Nimnad.

"Oh no I haven't." He replied to a surprised Lucy. "I'm not supposed to GIVE you luck to ORDER. There's supposed to be an element of CHANCE to it Lucy." He said, feeling rather defensive. Yet again Nim was beginning to feel more and more emotional as time was passing by.

"But this is embarrassing, and you COULD help me if you really wanted to." Lucy said, desperately.

"Well that's just it Lucy. I'm starting to feel as though I don't want to. I feel as though you are taking me for granted, and you have forgotten what a special gift you have been given." He said, hoping to jog her conscience. But it didn't work. Lucy just got angry and stormed off to the toilets. The little pink Nimnad didn't follow her, as she was beginning to make him feel very disappointed and so he watched the rest of the family continue to have fun whilst Lucy was gone.

When Lucy returned she tried casually walking through him as though she hadn't seen him, but he was so fed up about the way she thought she could use him as she pleased that he moved backwards very quickly so as to avoid her. She was amazed that he avoided her in that way and to her disgust, he accidentally stepped backwards through her uncle Ray!...... Poof! A puff of pink smoke and he was gone!...The Nimnad that was, not uncle Ray!

Totally oblivious to what was going on, uncle Ray stepped forward to pick up a bowling ball. As he placed his fingers and thumb in the holes to grip it, he realised that the ball he had picked up was too tight for his fingers. He tried to pull the ball off his hand but it wouldn't budge! He shook his hand furiously but his fingers must have swelled up inside the holes and the ball remained firmly fixed to the end of his hand!

The rest of the family began to giggle at the sight of him trying to remove the ball from his hand. It looked so funny, but as he turned to look at them they instantly changed their reaction from one of humour to one of concern. They were all too well aware that uncle Ray was not very good at taking criticism OR seeing the funny side of things when the joke was on him. Auntie Sue quickly moved to his aid to see if she could help him remove the afflicting bowling ball.... But it was going nowhere! She turned her head to look back at the rest of the family who were standing together in a group watching in anticipation, waiting to see what would happen next.

Well, uncle Ray looked so annoyed..... Auntie Sue looked so worried, and then suddenly, the rest of the family couldn't contain themselves any longer! They all burst out laughing! They laughed so much that they had tears rolling down their faces! (Lucy on the other hand was feeling a little guilty because she knew why her uncle had been so unlucky as to get the ball stuck on his hand in the first place.) That was it! Enough was enough for uncle Ray! He exploded in a temper tantrum and started flinging his arms around trying to get the ball to fall off. By now he had gathered quite an audience. He shook his arm so hard that he lost his balance and slipped. As he fell to the floor he banged his arm against the ball dispenser and it fell off. The ball that is.... Not his arm! The family watched, their mouths wide open, with a feeling of dread. As the ball rolled down the lane, the little pink Nimnad reappeared. This time he was actually clinging to the ball which had just left uncle Ray's hand and was tumbling round and round as the ball headed for the skittles. Lucy was desperate not to lose track of where Nim was going. The rest of the family were desperately trying not to lose track of where uncle Ray was going, because he was at that very moment, storming off to the bar to get a drink and sulk in a corner somewhere! They could only hope he would cheer up later on and try to see the funny side of it, although that wasn't very likely but there was no harm in hoping. Lucy, still preoccupied with the game, was watching the balls as they returned to the dispenser. Uncle Ray's ball closely accompanied by the Nimnad had completely missed all of the skittles and was due to reappear at any moment! So Lucy wasn't taking her eyes off the game. The family were returning their attentions to the game, however having made a joint decision to let Uncle Ray 'get on with it', and telling each other that, 'he'll get over it'.

"He always does." Lucy's dad said.

"Hey!" Lucy shouted to her cousins. "Come on, it's my turn!" All the family gathered to watch her. Lucy waited with excitement for Nim to appear from the dispenser. Just as she had expected, there he was! Still clinging to the ball as though he was moulded onto the side of it. Lucy grabbed it quickly before Nim had a chance to remove himself and...., POOF! He was gone again!

Most of uncle Ray's audience had re-formed back into groups and were now happily playing their own games, but Beth and her mates were still nosing around and keeping a watchful eye on Lucy's affairs. Lucy swung her arm back, took a moment to look in Beth's direction with a very smug look on her face and effortlessly let the ball go down the lane. STRIKE! All of the skittles went down! Lucy had got her own way after all. Beth and her lot looked on in amazement at the sudden transformation of Lucy's game.

Beth was not at all happy with Lucy's performance. In fact she was downright angry that Lucy had been able to play so well, and in front of the boy's too. Lucy continued to play well for the rest of the game and she noticed that gradually as the evening went on, the two boys who had accompanied Beth and Amber to the bowling alley were paying more and more attention to watching her. Whilst Beth and Amber giggled and showed off flirtatiously, the boys paid less and less attention to them, and were more interested in looking in Lucy's direction. Lucy couldn't believe it! She'd never had any attention from boys before. Not unless it was to laugh at her or watch Beth make a fool of her.

Lucy?..... taking the attentions of Beth's boyfriends? oh dear she would surely pay a very high price for that ... or would she?

Gradually the evening came to an end and the family filtered over to the desk to return their hired shoes. Uncle Ray casually strolled over to them from the direction of the bar as if nothing had happened, (thank goodness!) and Lucy carefully slid out of the door in uncle Ray's shadow in a bid not to be spotted by anyone that she didn't want to be spotted by.

MARBLES IN A JAR

Lucy woke up all bleary eyed at around 10am the next morning. She rolled over in her bed to check the time on her phone and suddenly realised that she hadn't seen Nim since the bowling alley! She shot out of bed like a rocket and began searching her bedroom for him, clambering over Leanne, who was asleep in a sleeping bag on her bedroom floor.

"What's the matter Lucy?" she asked, in a tired, half asleep, groaning kind of voice. "What you looking for?"

"Oh....., nothing. It's alright Leanne, go back to sleep." Lucy replied innocently. She was trying to think where she had last seen him, only she had become so wrapped up with her own self importance the night before that she hadn't even given Nim a second thought when they left the bowling alley.

Leanne curled up into a ball like a Caterpillar and drifted back into a deep sleep. Lucy continued to open her drawers and cupboards in an attempt to track down the Nimnad. When she realised that she wasn't going to find him in her room she gave up looking, put her dressing gown on over her PJ's and went downstairs to the kitchen to make some tea and toast. She sat down at the kitchen table and waited for the kettle to boil and the toast to pop up. Buddy was sitting beside her as he usually did, watching her every move attentively! Not, as you may assume for a cuddle but for his No 1 obsession – Food. Lucy listened for the little Nimnad to sneeze, but there was nothing.

She looked around the kitchen but he wasn't there. She went into the front room, but there was no sign of him in there either..... and still no sneezing. Now Lucy started to really worry that she may have lost him. How would she feel if she never saw him again? It didn't bear thinking about.

Just as she started to wander back into the kitchen, the doorbell rang. She turned towards the front door and walked towards it, wondering who it might be. Mum and dad must've gone out shopping with auntie Sue and uncle Ray, because there was no way they would all still be in bed! And it wouldn't be them as they would have a key to get in. She tied up the belt on her dressing gown, took hold of a barking Buddy by the collar in one hand, and opened the front door with the other. It was one of the boys from the bowling alley! You know the ones with Beth?

Lucy asked in a shy quiet voice, "oh hi, erm what'd you want?" then she turned her attention to Buddy and shouted at him, "STOP IT!" then she looked back up at the boy and asked him again. "What d'you want?" Buddy walked off sulking and climbed into his bed. The boy, (whom Lucy was thinking was very good looking!) held out his hand towards her. At this point her heart started Pounding. She thought that this must be a wind up and that he was going to reveal a horrible spider or something of a similar nasty nature and throw it at her! Instead he opened his hand to reveal a lucky horseshoe pendant on a neck chain. It was Lucy's! She'd been wearing it the previous night and the boy had found it on the floor where Lucy's family had been standing whilst playing their game. He wondered if it belonged to her or her cousin.

"Oh, that's mine. Where did you find it?" Lucy said in a shaky voice.

"It was on the floor where you were playing last night Lucy. That is your name isn't it?"

"Yeah." Lucy replied. "Well thanks anyway..... It's nice of you to drop it round." She smiled. The boy stood on Lucy's doorstep looking rather awkward as if he wanted to say something else.

"Is that all?" she asked, hoping that he might ask her to go out with him. So consumed with her own self importance that yet again she didn't notice Nim who was standing on the ground beside the potted conifer tree, to the side of the front door.

"Erm yeah, that's all. Bye." The boy said, as he couldn't pluck up the courage to ask her out.

Lucy dropped the necklace accidentally as she turned to go back in to the house, and as she bent down to pick it up she saw the Nimnad! Instead of being pleased to see him for the right reasons and asking him if he was ok. Or, even saying sorry for her inappropriate behaviour the night before. She selfishly made a grab for him and he disappeared again in a puff of pink smoke! Within seconds, the boy turned around, crossed back over the road and walked towards Lucy!

"Actually yeah, there is something I wanted to say." He said, looking more confident now.

"I was wondering if you'd like to go out with me sometime?" he stood in front of Lucy, waiting for a response. Lucy's stomach was doing somersaults as she breathed in so deeply that she struggled to get the words out of her mouth!

"Yeah..., that'd be great. Where do you want to go?" she smiled.

"Oh I dunno, maybe we could go to the cinema? What do you reckon?"

"Yes ok then." Lucy answered.

"Ok, I'll text you, what's your number?"
Lucy was in a state of shock as she gave him the number of her mobile. Things like this just didn't happen to her...., NOT EVER!!!

"By the way, my name's Sam!" he called out as he was walking away smiling. Lucy turned, walked back into her house and closed the front door just as Ryan appeared at the bottom of the stairs.

"Alright Luce?" he inquired. "Who was that?"

"Nothing important." She answered dismissively. "It was just someone doing a survey that's all." She didn't want him to know in case he embarrassed her.

"Where's mum and dad?" he asked, as he made his way over to the kitchen table with a box of Weetabix and a carton of milk.

"I don't know? Gone shopping I suppose." Said Lucy.
As Ryan was depositing four Weetabix into a large bowl, which he had just taken from the already washed crockery in the dishwasher, all four of the missing persons arrived home through the front door.

"Hi guys!" they called out. "We knew you wouldn't be up at the crack of dawn so we decided to pop out and do some early Christmas shopping." Said Mum.

"Oh! Did you get anything for me?" Ryan asked, with a cheeky grin on his face and raising his eyebrows up and down.

"Now that would be telling." His dad laughed.

"Well anyway, we'd better be making tracks and get our lazy little Herbert's out of bed," auntie Sue turned and looked at uncle Ray.

"Yes you're right love," he sighed as he browsed over the front page of his newspaper.

"Ok kids! Come on...! Get yourselves up and dressed, we're going soon!" he shouted up the stairs. By which time, mum was making a nice cuppa for everyone and Ryan was working his way through his last Weetabix. After a short while Lucy and Ryan's cousins came down stairs dressed and ready to go, and they all sat down in the kitchen together, chatting and laughing about the previous night at the bowling alley. Even uncle Ray had to smile to himself for getting so annoyed over a bowling ball! About an hour or so later they all said their goodbyes and auntie, uncle, and cousins left to go home.

Dad went outside in the garden to get the hose out so he could wash the car, mum went around gathering up any washing that she could find, and Lucy and Ryan retreated back upstairs to their rooms.

Lucy sat on her bed staring into space thinking about the night before and about Sam. Every now and then she would look at her mobile as she was still waiting for him to text her. She decided to ask Ryan if he would go with her to Bluewater shopping centre to look around and get some ideas for Christmas presents as she never liked to go on her own, just in case she bumped into Beth. She opened her wardrobe and took out a box which had some make up in it. Just some light blue eye shadow, mascara and a lip gloss. She put a little on and was posing in the mirror, when she noticed Nim in the reflection behind her. He was sitting on her bed looking very sad. Lucy turned and looked at him for a moment.

"Hi Nim," she said, feeling a little uncomfortable. The reason Lucy didn't feel the same towards him now was because she had turned all of her attentions onto herself. She had become totally self absorbed and SHE was now the most important thing in her world.

"Alright Lucy?" asked Nim. "How are you today?" Instead of taking the time to remember how lucky she was to have met the Nimnad and appreciate his kindness, she went straight into how she was going to Bluewater shopping centre, and how she was going to make Ryan go with her. You've got to come with me too Nim, just in case I need you." She told him.

The little Nimnad felt in his heart that he should take himself away from Lucy as she no longer deserved him because of the way she was behaving. He wondered whether he should go to see the Great Nimnad and tell him what was happening. But instead, he decided to go with her to Bluewater, (even though he didn't really like water!) in the hopes that he could make Lucy see what was happening to her in the process of becoming more confident and receiving more good luck.

"Ok Lucy, I'll come too." He agreed."

"Great," she said, as she busily got herself ready. When Ryan and Lucy were both ready they said goodbye to mum, having already checked it was ok for them to go, and left the house.

"Bye dad, see you later!" they called out loudly so that he could hear them above the noise of the hosepipe gushing water out all over the car. The car that dad took so much pride in and took such good care of because it was the family car, their only car and, "cars cost money you know?" that's what dad would say to them when they complained about the fact that their car was too old and not trendy enough. Of course Lucy's dad would love a fancy car but at the present time it was out of the question. Even with mum's winnings they couldn't afford it. Credit cards to pay off, and Christmas coming too! It was an expensive time of year for everyone.

After about an hour's ride on the bus, they arrived at Bluewater. It was a big place, set down in a dip surrounded by chalk cliffs. All the shops were inside, under one roof and it looked especially pretty at this time of year as it was dressed with an array of pretty fairy lights and luxurious decorations hung from the ceiling, making the whole place look like a massive grotto. Lucy and Ryan got off the bus followed by Nim.

"Where shall we go first?" Ryan asked as he looked around for the nearest entrance to the centre.

"Let's go to the Gadget shop first." He said.

"Ok, but don't walk so fast Ryan," replied Lucy as she struggle to keep up with him. As they entered the shopping centre the first thing they saw was a giant sweet jar, about three metres tall and it was full of marbles all different colours and patterns. There was a competition and the prize was a brand new Aston Martin convertible car. There was a big sign next to the jar that read, 'Guess the marbles in the jar and win an Aston Martin car!'

"Oh my god! Look at that car Ryan!" Lucy said excitedly.

"That is sooo sick....., Dad would love that." Ryan answered as he gazed at the beautiful car.

"Dad?" Lucy looked at Ryan as if he had lost HIS marbles.

"What about us?" she said to him in disbelief that he had even considered not having it all to himself if he won it. "Could you imagine going to school in that?" she continued. Without hesitation, she looked around for the Nimnad, saw him down beside her feet and reached down and made a grab for him. In a puff of pink smoke he was gone!

"That should do it." She said as she strode over to the lady who was standing beside the 'Guess the marbles in the jar' sign. The competition was being sponsored by Kiss radio station. They had a DJ there and everything! Even flashing lights and music being played very loudly. It was all very exciting.

Unbeknown to Lucy and Ryan, Beth and her mates were also at Bluewater and had been hanging around the competition area all afternoon. Between Beth and her mates, which consisted of Justine Jackson, Carley Campbell, Sam (what the hell was HE doing there with Beth? Holding hands too!) plus a couple of other boys, who she'd never seen before. They had spent over twenty pounds trying to guess the number of marbles in the jar.

"Oooh! Look who it is." Beth sniggered to her mates whilst looking Lucy up and down as if she had just crawled out from under a stone. Lucy and Ryan just stood still looking at the floor at first as they didn't want to look Beth in the eye. If either of them looked her in the eye she would probably find that reason enough to pick on Lucy even more. Anyway, Lucy suddenly remembered that she had Nim at her side! She raised her head up and looked Beth and the others straight in the eye. Ryan was watching Lucy now and wondering what on earth she was playing at. Beth was standing right there in front of her, still holding hands with Sam, who was saying nothing to help Lucy!

After knocking on Lucy's front door and having asked her out, he had the nerve to stand there in front of her, holding hands with Beth whilst Beth insulted her! Lucy felt a wave of anger surge through her! She turned and walked in the direction of the lady with the microphone and said,

"I'm ready to guess."

"Ok!" The lady said, loudly into the microphone. "We have another contestant for guess the marbles in a jar and win a car!"

"And your name is?" the Lady asked.

"Lucy Miles," she replied in a very precise and clear voice.

"Oooh!" Beth's lot called out.

"And how many marbles do you think are in the jar Lucy?" the lady asked, holding the microphone up to Lucy's face now waiting for an answer.

"17,924." Lucy replied. Just like that, she didn't stop to think about it, she just opened her mouth and said it. A few moments of silence followed, and then the stunned DJ played a fanfare. Confetti cannons of all different colours erupted and lights flashed! Everyone involved in the competition suddenly seemed very excited.

"You've won Lucy!" the lady shouted into the microphone.

"Lucy Miles you have just won yourself a brand new top of the range Aston Martin convertible car!" she said very loudly over the microphone so that everyone in Bluewater could hear. You should have seen the look on Beth's face! If looks could kill, Lucy would have dropped to the floor right there and then.

"Oh my god Ryan!" Lucy shouted. "We've won it! We've won it! We've won the car!"

Ryan, bless him just stood there staring at the car with his eyes and mouth wide open. Obviously there would be a matter of paperwork to be filed in and Lucy's mum and dad would have to be contacted due to the fact that Lucy was too young to drive. But for the moment, she was lapping up the attention of being in the spotlight for the right reason for a change, and it felt so good to get one up on Beth and her lot too.

"I bet Sam wishes it was MY hand he was holding now?" She thought to herself. Lucy and Ryan jumped up and down and hugged each other with joy and excitement. They were laughing and Lucy felt happier than she had done for a very long time. Until Beth appeared beside Lucy, backed by her mates, including Sam! "You're such a BITCH! You cheat!" shouted Beth, and with both hands she pushed Lucy's shoulders causing Lucy to stumble and fall backwards. Lucy turned her head to see what was behind her. She could see electrical cables and light stands. She couldn't stop herself from falling. It all happened so quickly, and then she landed, smack on her bum! She was behind the safety barrier that was in front of the cables and leads. The barrier was now lying on the floor because Lucy had knocked it over as she fell. She stood up and as she went to move away, she caught her foot in what she thought was a power cable. She gave it an almighty yank and then heard a rumbling noise. That was when she realised that it wasn't a power cable at all! It was actually a safety line which must have been attached to the giant jar so that nobody could tamper with it! The line was designed to anchor the jar to the floor! The jar was now wobbling as though trying to decide whether or not to fall over! There was such a fuss going on around Beth that no one noticed Lucy giving the jar a helping hand in making a decision which way to go! She gave it a huge shove in Beth's direction, and it toppled right over! Suddenly there came an avalanche of marbles rolling around all over the place. Beth couldn't stand up because she was constantly falling over on them. Her mates who had tried to do a runner were also falling all over the place. Arms and legs were waving about in all directions! Two security officers were making their way over to Beth in an attempt not to fall over. Lucy thought they looked like they'd wet themselves! She could have got into a lot of trouble if anyone had seen her adding the final touches to this disaster but she wanted so much to burst out laughing at the sight before her. She managed to keep a straight face though and watch the whole fiasco with the same look of astonishment as her brother.

When everyone had stopped falling over and all the marbles were still, it was Beth who got the blame for the whole episode of events!

Lucy had won a dream car, and got her own back on Beth and Sam. She had come out on top of it all, looking really good. Unfortunately, in managing to feel so good, she hadn't realised that yet again poor little Nim had been treated with utter disrespect, and had even been forgotten about. He hadn't re-appeared yet and Lucy hadn't even noticed. Lucy, Lucy, Lucy... that's all that was on her mind right now! She couldn't wait to get to school on Monday to see everyone's reaction to her fabulous win and of course..................., the reaction to what had happened to Beth! For the first time in a long while, Lucy was actually looking forward to going to school.

Having asked Lucy for her side of the story AND spoken

to Beth, the security officers left the scene. They had however given Beth a verbal warning that if her name appeared to be attached to any incident of this nature again, that she would be taking a trip to the local police station and barred from Bluewater. You can imagine how well that went down with Beth!

The manager of the competition came over to see Lucy, who, by now, was now standing with Ryan beside the brand spanking new Aston Martin car.

"We are so sorry about that Lucy. Are you ok?" the manager asked. "Do you know that girl?"

"Yes," Lucy said. "She goes to my school." She continued with a look of complete innocence on her face!

"Well as long as you are ok now?" the manager enquired.

Lucy looked at Ryan and they both looked at the car. They took a deep breath and replied with a delightedly happy, "YES."

"Let's give your parents a call to tell them the good news shall we?" he asked. And he started to call the number from his mobile that Lucy had given him. Lucy and Ryan were overcome with excitement!

"Is that Mr Miles?" the manager asked.

"Yes, Mr Miles speaking." He said.

The manager went on to explain how Lucy had won the car and the sequence of events that had followed with Beth and the security officers. Within minutes Lucy's mum and dad were in their car and on their way to the shopping centre! When they arrived they dashed straight to where the competition had been. There, sitting in the car were Lucy and Ryan!

"Hi kids!" mum called out. They had beaming smiles on their faces.

"WOW!" dad shouted. "Is this the car?" he asked.

"Don't be silly dad, it's that old banger parked outside in the car park." Ryan said as he laughed.

"It's awesome isn't it?" Lucy said.

"God yeah, it's gorgeous." Mum replied.

"It's the business." Dad declared. "Is this REALLY ours?" he asked with a look of disbelief on his face.

"Yes dad!" Ryan replied with a raised voice. "Come on dad, get in!" he continued.

"Is that Ok?" dad looked at the manager who was watching the family enjoy the excitement of winning the car.

"Of course sir," said the manager. "It's yours now, well........., I mean Lucy's." He said with a smile on his face. "Go ahead sir," he said as he stretched his arm out in the direction of the beautiful car.

The car was jet black, and so shiny that it was like looking into a mirror! The seats were soft and comfy and covered with white leather. The roof was folded down at the back and was made from a soft material.

"Come on dad, get in then." Ryan said. "It's like James Bond's car." He said breathlessly, he was so excited.

"Ooh, isn't it lovely?" mum remarked as she watched dad get into the car. "It smells so clean and new."

"It's the leather seats love," said dad. "Come on then, you getting in?" he asked her.

The manager walked around to the other side of the car from the passenger side to where Lucy was sitting in the driver's seat. Ryan was beside her in the front passenger seat. Mum and dad were in the back!

The manager leaned into the car and put the key into a slot on the dashboard. Even the key was special. It looked a bit like a miniature credit card and was very light to hold.

"Now then," he said to Ryan. "If you push that button...." and he pointed to a button down by the gear stick. Before he'd a chance to finish what he was saying, Lucy had already pushed it! The roof began to unfold itself and lift up from the back!

"That's wicked!" Ryan shouted as he watched the roof closing over the top of them all. The manager was not impressed by Lucy's behaviour at all. She was now fiddling around with the stereo, which was up way too loud as well!

"Turn it down love!" mum was trying to be heard above the noise of the stereo.

"Alright alright!" Lucy snapped back at her mum. Dad tried to rise above Lucy's rudeness and just kept repeating how fantastic it was that the car had parking sensors....., as mum wasn't very good at parking! The manager leaned into the car again and switched the ignition off, once the roof had closed. He found the whole experience very disappointing. And mum was very embarrassed by Lucy's behaviour too.

A GOOD DAY

Having spent the rest of Sunday filing out papers and bringing the new car home, the day had passed very quickly. It wasn't until Sunday night when going to bed that Lucy realised she hadn't seen Nim for ages again. In fact she hadn't seen him since the fiasco at Bluewater. Yet again, she had been so full of herself and the car that she had completely forgotten about him. Oh dear! What was happening to Lucy? With all of her success she seemed to be losing something.

"Oh well, he'll turn up again soon I expect." Lucy thought to herself very flippantly, and off she went to bed. She had already said good night to her family. She'd also persuaded her mum to go sick and finish work early the next day so that she could pick Lucy up from school in the new car. SHE wanted to show off! She didn't even consider her brother and how excited he must've been too. The only thing that Lucy was thinking about now was LUCY. She was becoming very selfish and ruthless.........., not qualities she'd ever admired in other people.

Monday morning came and Lucy dragged herself out of bed and went to the bathroom to have a wash and brush her teeth.

"Morning," she grunted at her brother as they passed each other on the landing. Ryan was on his way back from the bathroom having been ready for school for about twenty minutes already. He had just put the final touches to his hair with some moulding putty. He was really looking forward to telling his mates at school about their win at the weekend.

And everything else that had happened!

Lucy on the other hand was now on a complete ego trip and was full of herself and 'HER CAR!' and 'HER NIMNAD!' and, 'HER GOOD LUCK!'

"Bye mum!" Ryan called out as he left the house to make his way to school. He didn't bother calling out to his sister as he didn't expect to get an answer from her, and he didn't wait for her because he actually DID care about getting to school on time..... Unlike Lucy.

"Bye love." His mum replied. "Have a good day!" she called out as he walked out of the front door, and off he went. Dad had already left for work ages ago. Mum was quickly finishing off a slice of toast and a slurp of cold tea before she headed off for work when Lucy descended down the stairs. Tired as usual but something was different. There was an inner confidence radiating from her. She had an heir of authority that she didn't usually have. Lucy was changing. "Don't forget you're picking me up from school today mum, in MY Aston." she said sarcastically, without even eye contacting her mum. It came across as more of a demand than a reminder!

She bent down to reach for her school bag, took her packed lunch from the kitchen table, (which her mum had lovingly made for her) and didn't even bother to say thanks. Then she turned and headed down the hallway towards the front door and opened it. There he was! Sitting on top of a terracotta plant pot, which mum had turned upside down the day before so that it wouldn't fill up with water if it rained, (she had emptied it ready to plant some fresh winter pansies in there), was Nim! Loyal as ever....., waiting to escort Lucy to school!

"Oh there you are." she said, as if he was now more of an irritation than an asset. Lucy said to Nim, in a more irritated fashion rather than being relieved that he had appeared to her again safe and sound.

"Hello Lucy," he said. "How are you today?"

"I'm great....." She paused as she pulled the front door shut behind her. "I've won a fabulous new car and mum's picking me up from school in it tonight. Come on let's hurry up and get to school. I can't wait to see how jealous Beth is going be." Lucy opened the gate, hurried through it and slammed it shut behind her without a care for the Nimnad. She didn't even look back to make sure he was still with her. She just assumed he would be, seeing as he was for HER convenience only! Poor little Nim partly ran and partly hovered along beside her all the way to school. There was no conversation and no words were exchanged until they were in sight of the school gate. Lucy was different. The Nimnad had noticed a big change in her. She was very sure of herself now and didn't seem to be scared of anyone anymore.

"Right... stay by me today Nim," said Lucy. "I don't want anyone else getting near you, you're mine and that's the way we are going to keep it alright?"
The gentleness that had radiated from Lucy when the Nimnad first met her was gone. She had a harshness about her now and it wasn't nice. As the pair of them drew nearer to the school gate Lucy found herself feeling vindictive and

started plotting to think of ways she could get revenge on Beth and her lot. There she was. Lucy could see Beth across the playground, she was standing with some sixth form boys and a couple of her mates and they were all chatting to each other. Although Lucy's school was a girl's school, there were always boys in the sixth form who had transferred from boy's schools that didn't have a sixth form of their own. Beth was sipping at a cup of hot chocolate that she had bought from the breakfast bar in the school canteen. Beyond where Beth was standing Lucy could see a group of boys playing football with a large sponge ball. It was at that very moment Lucy decided exactly what was going to happen to Beth!

"Come on Nim," Lucy whispered to the Nimnad.

"Where are we going Lucy?" he asked.

"Just be quiet and hurry up. Follow me," she ordered. (Not that anybody else could hear him!)
Anyway, she hurried across the playground making sure to stay by the edge in the hopes that she might not be noticed too soon, told the Nimnad to follow quickly, and moved very closely past the boy who was trying to defend a make believe goal post. Lucy rushed past the boy so quickly that he turned to see what she was doing, calling after her.

"Hey! Watch where ya going ya stupid idiot!" as he turned back to his game he collided with the Nimnad.........
Poof!...... Nim was gone in a puff of pink smoke! The ball was heading straight for the goal as the boy tripped over his shoe lace which had come undone, he totally missed the ball, and it bounced past him..........., and yes...., you guessed it!

The ball hit Beth right in the back of the head just as she was about to take a sip of her hot chocolate! Beth's arm was jolted across her body and the cup followed the path her arm had taken, leaving only one possible outcome! Yes!...... HOT CHOCOLATE ALL OVER BETH'S FACE!!!

It was up her nose and dripping from her eyelashes. Beth was not amused. In fact she was positively fuming! She marched straight over to the boys to have a go at them, but immediately wished she hadn't because one of them was Sam......... Oh no! How embarrassing! She was beginning to get a taste of her own medicine, which must have felt pretty good to Lucy, but the way she was going about it was not so good because she was now abusing the little Nimnad and everything that his utter existence stood for.

Beth turned away with her head down and walked quietly to the girl's toilets to clean herself up. Even her mates were laughing, although they were trying not to let her see in case she took her anger out on them later. They were not used to seeing their leader on the wrong end of her own type of tricks, and they were beginning to see her in a different light. Having been led by her and almost in awe of her strength of character for so long, they were now beginning to realise that actually.... On her own, she was not as big and strong as she pretended to be when she had all of her gang around her to back her up. Lucy had been watching all of this happen from afar. It gave her great pleasure. She began to cast her eyes around to look for the Nimnad. And there he was! She could see him wandering towards her from across the school playing field. He didn't have a spring in his step anymore. Nor could he even be bothered to hover. He looked very depressed, but Lucy didn't notice at all. All she could see now when she looked at Nim was a useful tool to help her gain power and respect, which was something she had not felt at school for a long time if at all. The point she was missing was the fact that she really didn't need to have power. She was confusing not wanting to be bullied anymore with having power over others and if she wasn't careful she would end up becoming a very unhappy girl for completely different reasons to the ones at the beginning of this story.

The school bell rang across the playground and everyone started to move towards the school building. Lucy waited back awhile so that she could grab Nim as he arrived beside her. He looked up at Lucy with very heavy eyes and before he could say anything she made a grab for him. POOF! He was gone!

"That should set me up for a good morning." She thought.

Registration came and went without any dramas and the whole morning was booked out for a science lesson. Lucy actually did enjoy science, because it was one of the few subjects that she didn't have any difficulty learning and remembering. She knew she was good at it. Unfortunately she didn't have any mates in her science class and the whole of Beth's lot were in that class together, including Beth! She managed to get by though because she always sat at the front near the teacher.

Mrs Fogarty the science teacher was very slim with a tiny waist and long straight brown hair. She was very softly spoken and seemed quite fragile and yet the girl's instinctively knew not to mess with her as there was an underlying feeling that there was another side to her that she could quite easily bring to light should the need arise. The girl's made their way to the lab and formed a queue outside. The corridor was awash with the hustle and bustle of bodies rushing around making their way to their due destination. The air was full of the humming of voices as the girls chatted and giggled and went on their way. Gradually the corridor emptied of moving bodies and there was just a stationary queue waiting for Mrs Fogarty, who was walking at a steady pace towards them. They quietened down and watched her. She was wearing a calf length orange and brown flowery tiered skirt with a brown v necked tee shirt. She had flat brown leather strappy sandals on and was carrying a large holdall bag which looked as though it was housing some school books, (probably homework to be marked!)   In the other hand, she was carrying a brown leather briefcase.

"Good morning girls," she softly greeted them. "Right," she said as she opened the door to the lab.

"Come in and sit yourselves down at your own places." She made her way over to her desk at the front of the class and opened up her briefcase, removed some papers from it, closed it and placed it on the floor beside her chair. There was a slight hum drum of voices from girl's muttering under their breath to each other.

"Ok, ok!" Mrs Fogarty said loudly, which was the closest the girl's had ever heard to a shout from her.

"Today we are going to conduct an experiment.... You will need to take out your Bunsen burners, test tubes and holders from your cupboards. I will be bringing round some chemicals for each of you and I shall explain what we will be doing with them in a minute." She said whilst removing some more papers from her holdall. She looked up and continued.

"Justine Jackson and Carley Campbell, I know you like to work together but for the purpose of this experiment I'm afraid I am going to split you up." The two girls frowned at each other.

"I want to know that every result is individual and there has been no copying of results." Mrs Fogarty said, as she browsed around the lab.

"Lucy...., for the duration of this lesson only, can you swap places with Carley please?" Although Mrs Fogarty asked Lucy as if she had a choice about whether or not she moved, Lucy knew that she didn't really have a choice. Mrs Fogarty was just telling her to move but in a very polite manner. And not wanting to seem un-obliging, the pair of them gathered up their belongings and wandered over to each other's place straight away. Lucy's stomach churned at the sight of Beth sitting directly behind her, Justine to her left and Carley was in front, just across to the right a bit, in LUCY'S SEAT. She was gutted that she'd been moved. She sat staring at her patch of the lab table for a moment, sulking, and then, as she looked down at her bag on the floor, she noticed out of the corner of her eye, sitting on the floor over by the window, was Nim! He waved at her, smiling hopefully for Lucy to be pleased to see him. But instead it just reminded her that she was due a nice big chunk of good luck and how she could use HIM to get it. She quickly beckoned him over to her as she didn't want anyone else to get near him. She leaned down and pretended to take something out of her bag.

"Get under my bag so that no one can get near you Nim," she whispered. The little Nimnad did as he was told. In fact he lay down under her bag and closed his eyes. He wanted to fall asleep. He didn't want to be a part of this anymore. He had never experienced feelings of sadness like this before and as he laid there underneath Lucy's bag with his eyes closed, a single tear formed in the corner of Nim's eye, gently trickled down his cheek and dripped onto the floor.

"Ok ladies," said Mrs Fogarty. "Today we are going to define the properties of ...." and so she went on. Mrs Fogarty's voice became a drone of 'bla bla bla' as Lucy cooked up a plan in her head to make Beth look really stupid in front of her mates again.

"When I light my Bunsen burner I want you all to come to the front of the class and stand around my desk. I want you to watch what I do girl's," continued Mrs Fogarty. "When I have shown you all how to conduct this experiment and the outcome that you will be expected to have at the end, I want you to go back to your place and prepare the apparatus. (They're the things they use for the experiment!)

By the time the demonstration was finished it was time for break and at the sound of the bell the girls down tooled and left the lab in a hurry. All except for Lucy, and the little Nimnad, who incidentally was still doing as he had been told and was lying on the floor underneath Lucy's bag.

"Do you mind if I stay in for break Miss? Lucy asked.

"You can if you like?" replied Mrs Fogarty, as if she were asking. "What do you want to do that for?"
Lucy knew she would be far better off indoors reading than outside at the mercy of that lot. Even if staying indoors reading may result in them calling her a geek!

"Thanks Miss." Said Lucy enthusiastically, as she sat down at her place and pretended to start reading a book. Mrs Fogarty gathered up her bags and said, "I'm just popping out for a quick coffee Lucy. I shan't be long. Will you be ok?"

"Yes Miss." Lucy said, studiously looking at the front page of her text book.

"Well don't touch anything, ok? See you in a minute." Mrs Fogarty said in a trusting voice and hurried off out of the lab to the staff room for coffee.

As luck would have it, Mrs Fogarty in her haste, had left the key to the chemicals cupboard on her desk! "Great!" Thought Lucy, and she quickly opened up the cupboard, having made sure that no one was coming. She replaced the powdery substance which was sitting in the bottom of Beth's test tube with a different one of a very similar colour, only this one was of an explosive nature when heated!

"Oh yes, that bitch is gonna get it!" Lucy thought to herself. "This is going to be great!" she told herself as she conjured up a picture of Beth with black soot all over her face and her hair standing on end. She quickly locked the cupboard again and placed the key back on Mrs Fogarty's desk where it had been left. She returned to where she had been sitting and continued to pretend to read her book. Very soon the bell was ringing and everybody was returning to the lab, including Mrs Fogarty, still clutching a half empty mug of coffee. All of the girls made their way back to their places very quickly without having to be told, as this was the part of the lesson that they enjoyed! Getting stuck in, they all began setting up their test tubes and lighting there Bunsen burners.

"OK!!" Mrs Fogarty actually shouted!
The girls quietened down so that she could be heard.

"You all know what you are supposed to be doing, so off you go. I'll be walking round to observe you and if anybody has any problems just put your hand up and I will come and see you." She said in a softer voice.

The girls began to slowly heat the chemicals in their test tubes over the flame of the Bunsen Burner. The idea was that it should gradually change colour from a pale grey to a deep red colour and then crystallise. Everybody was happy with the progress theirs was making, except Beth. Hers wasn't doing anything! Lucy kept a close watch on her from the corner of her eye as she kept subtly glancing sideways.

"Miss!" Beth called out, impatiently. "Miss! Mine's not doing anything?" she said, sounding genuinely inquisitive and looking puzzled.

"Be patient Beth,"

Mrs Fogarty was used to Beth's anti social behaviour and paid no attention to her quiery. She assumed that Beth was up to her usual games and generally seeking attention.

Beth moved her head closer to get a better look inside the test tube and noticed that the chemical was beginning to bubble.

SUDDENLY....................... BOOM!!!

There was an explosion in Beth's test tube! The glass broke and Beth's face was engulfed in a cloud of black smoke!

"BLOODY HELL!" Justine shouted, as she saw what had happened to Beth.

"Language Justine!!!" Mrs Fogarty really shouted now!

"Sorry Miss." She said.

"OMG! What was that?" Carley asked.

"Are you ok?" Amber joined in from behind.

Beth was in shock! That was the last thing she expected to happen! By now, Mrs Fogarty had made her way over to Beth and was checking that she was alright. Beth's face was covered in black soot and her hair was a mess. Lucy was overjoyed with the results but the Nimnad felt really disappointed that he had been used in this way again.

As soon as they realised Beth was alright the girls began to see the funny side of what had happened and an infectious laughter began to spread around the lab. Even Beth's friends couldn't stop giggling at the sight of her. Beth began to get really angry and she looked straight at Lucy.

"Right, settle down girls," said Mrs Fogarty. She spoke in a soft voice again now as she tried to bring calmness and order back in to the lab.

"Something has obviously gone wrong with Beth's experiment."

"Yeah you can say that again!" Justin couldn't contain herself and she lost it! With that, the whole class burst out laughing again! Beth was not happy at all.... Lucy was over the moon!

"Ok that's enough!" shouted Mrs Fogarty. Beth was looking quite helpless at this point. "I'm going to take Beth to the first aid room and I want you all to turn off your Bunsen burners and clear your apparatus away. When I come back I expect you all to be sitting quietly, writing up your findings in your exercise books Ok?" she added "Ok" at the end in order to get a response from the girls to make sure that they were listening to her instructions.

"Yes Miss!" they all said en-masse loudly.

Beth quietly left the lab with Mrs Fogarty. The tables had been completely turned! It was from that moment that Beth began to lose control of her friends. They started to make their own decisions and they began to realise that they actually quite liked Lucy, AND that she wasn't the annoying person that Beth had led everyone to believe!

The rest of the day passed quickly and calmly, Beth had been sent home for the afternoon and it was soon time to go home for everyone else too. The school bell was ringing through the classrooms and everyone busily packed their belongings into their bags in order to vacate the premises as quickly as possible.

Lucy couldn't wait for her mum to arrive at school in the new car! She had butterflies in her stomach because she was so excited at the thought of how jealous the other girls would be when they saw her getting into it. She rushed to the school gates as quickly as she could, and there parked up at the curb side right outside the school gates, was her mum in the new car. It was gleaming with newness and really stood out amongst the other cars outside the school. The weather was bright and dry so Lucy's mum had put the top down and it made the car look even classier!

"Wow!" Lucy could hear some girls saying.
Lucy stepped towards the car, and said, "Hi mum." With her head held high and looking very proud.

"Hello love. Jump in then, we might just be in time to pick Ryan up as well."
Lucy got into the car, grinning all over her face. Just as her mum was about to drive away Amber and Kerry came out of the school gate.

"Bye Lucy! See you tomorrow!" they called to her. They were obviously very impressed by the new car. She smiled and gave them a wave.

"Made some new friends love?" Mum asked.

"Yes." said Lucy, feeling very satisfied with herself.

"Hey Lucy!" a voice called from across the road. She looked up and saw Sam waving to her. "Wait a minute!" he called out. Lucy's first instinct was to ignore him as she was still angry, and a little hurt, if she was honest, about him being hand in hand with Beth at Bluewater. But then she looked up at him and remembered how nice it had felt when he had come to her house that day to return her necklace. She waited for him to weave his way across the road amongst the traffic.

"Yeah, what do you want?" Lucy asked him with a dismissive attitude.

"Erm well, I wanted to say sorry about me being with Beth at Bluewater." He said awkwardly.

"I didn't know you were going out together?" Lucy enquired.

"We're not," Sam replied. "It's just that Beth asked me out and I didn't know how to say no to her, so I went. She really likes me, but I didn't want to go out with her... I want to go out with you." Sam said as he blushed.

"Come on Lucy, hurry up or we'll miss Ryan!" Mum said.

"Ok hang on a minute." Said Lucy as she glared at her mum.

"D'you still want to go to the cinema then?" Sam asked her.

"Yeah." she said quickly.

"What about tonight then. I could come round for you at seven. Is that ok?" he asked.

"Yeah, ok then." Lucy nodded as mum pulled away.

Nim had been quietly following Lucy around and was

now sitting in the foot well of the car by Lucy's feet looking and feeling very sad. He wondered what he should do about the situation that he was finding himself in with Lucy. This was not what he had intended to happen at all and he was sure that her behaviour had not been part of the Great Nimnad's plan either. They drove by her brother's school just in time to catch everybody coming out and there was plenty of time for Lucy to show off. Nim stayed in the foot well whilst Lucy stepped out of the car and was leaning on the side of the bonnet with one eye on her mobile pretending to text and the other eye on the boys looking over the road at the car. Mum was watching out for Ryan as he wasn't expecting her to be there and he might miss a ride in the new car otherwise.

After about 10 minutes Ryan came walking out of the school gates chatting away to a friend. He didn't see mum and Lucy parked across the road, so mum hit the horn and he looked over to see who it was. His eyes lit up and he brought his friend across the road to get a closer look at the car. After showing the car off to his friend Ryan said goodbye to him and went to get into the car.

"What do you think you're doing?" Lucy asked, as Ryan opened the front passenger door.

"Erm, getting in the car?" he answered, looking puzzled and irritated by her attitude towards him.

"Oh no you're not," she replied. "I'M sitting in the front of MY car"

"OH WHATEVER!" not wanting to argue with his sister in

front of an ever growing audience as the boys came out of school, he gave in immediately and jumped into the back. If Lucy hadn't become so selfish she would have realised that she was embarrassing her brother and she would have let him sit in the front seat. After all she'd had her moment of glory outside HER school, BUT, everything was about Lucy now and she didn't have a thought for anyone else. During the drive home, Lucy's mum tried to explain to her how selfishly she had behaved towards Ryan but she shrugged it off as if both her mum and her brother were over reacting and no more was said about it.

Nim was devastated by the effect that he'd had on Lucy's personality. He struggled with himself to discover what he had done wrong. But he couldn't find the answer. All he did know was that Lucy was now beginning to behave just like the girls who had upset her so much before.

When they arrived home, mum, Lucy and Ryan all got out of the car in silence. Nim stayed in the foot well as he had decided he didn't want to accompany Lucy indoors. He waited until they had all gone in and then he climbed out of the car.

LUCY'S DATE

Sam arrived at Lucy's house promptly at 7pm. He rang the doorbell and Lucy's mum answered the door.

"Hello love." she said to him, with a welcoming smile on her face. "You must be Sam?"

"Yeah, is she ready?" Sam asked, almost tripping over his words with an heir of awkwardness about him that radiated down the hallway to where Lucy's dad was sitting in the kitchen reading his newspaper. He looked round to see Sam standing in the front doorway by Lucy's mum.

"Hiya!" he called out in an attempt to put Sam at his ease. "D'you want to come in here and wait for Lucy mate?" dad continued. "Cold out isn't it?"

"Yeah it is, alright then....Thanks." Sam answered politely. Whilst Sam was becoming acquainted with Lucy's dad, Lucy was upstairs frantically checking her hair and makeup. Pouting and smiling at herself in the mirror.

"Lucy!" Mum called upstairs. "Sam's here! Are you ready?"
Lucy quickly had one last check in the mirror. She was wearing a pair of dark blue denim jeggings with a pretty pink and silver sweatshirt and a pair of black suede ankle boots. As she descended down the stairs her mum remarked.

"Ooh, you look nice love." Lucy shushed her mum to be quiet and whispered in her ear not to embarrass her. Mum gave her a nod and a knowing smile. Then Lucy ushered her mum down the hallway as she called to Sam that she was ready. She didn't want to go into the kitchen where her dad was sitting, chatting to Sam because she was afraid that he might say something silly that WOULD DEFINITELY embarrass her. Sam said a polite goodbye to Lucy's parents and he and Lucy left the house together. As they walked and talked they discussed what sort of films they liked and what they should watch at the cinema. After much debating they decided on a comedy about some High School kids that get lost on a School trip.

The two of them chose to walk to the cinema as they had plenty of time and anyway, they were enjoying each other's company. During their journey Lucy was aware of random Nimnads on the way and she did her best to make sure Sam avoided two pink ones. On one occasion she 'accidently on purpose' bumped into him and knocked him sideways as if she had lost her balance as she walked. At one stage of their journey, the two of them were crossing the road at a zebra crossing and Sam started heading straight towards a pink Nimnad! In order to make him miss it, Lucy took hold of his hand and led him around the outside of the crossing over to the other side of the road.

"What did you do that for?" he asked, looking confused.

"You could have got me run over." He continued.

"Oh! Erm..., there was some dog's poo on the crossing and I didn't want you to tread in it." Lucy replied, in the hopes that he would believe her. Sam gave a slow nod of the head with a puzzled look on his face and carried on walking. As they continued towards the cinema, Lucy suddenly realised she was still holding Sam's hand, which made her feel good, and he didn't seem to mind, seeing as he hadn't let go of her hand either! She even pretended to trip over, which gave her the excuse that she needed to fall against him so as to knock him out of the path of an oncoming pink Nimnad! She was trying very hard not to let him have any bad luck!

Lucy did begin to worry that Sam might think she was a weirdo because of the way she had behaved on the way to the cinema. They had discovered that they had quite a lot in common and they DID get along VERY well but she still worried that he might think her a little odd! So....., she decided to let nature take its course and leave Sam's encounters with the Nimnads down to fate for the time being. Lucy decided that it wasn't her place to balance the luck in people's lives for them after all, and that she should leave well alone. Besides anything else, it had all become a bit too stressful!

By the time they reached the cinema after about a thirty minute walk, they felt quite well acquainted with each other. Sam offered to pay for Lucy's ticket but she insisted on paying for herself. She wanted to remain independent just in case she and Sam fell out with each other for any reason. She had got used to keeping her guard up. She didn't want to be beholden to him for anything..... Just in case he didn't turn out to be as nice as he seemed in the first instance. After all, he HAD previously hung around with Beth and her friends. And although Lucy now knew that Beth's friends weren't the scary threat that she'd once thought they were, she still felt a little uneasy about the situation. In fact the more Lucy thought about how hurt she'd felt when she saw Sam with

Beth at Bluewater, the more she couldn't resist the urge to use her vision for Nimnads to her advantage again!

They entered the cinema through a door that was open amongst a group of about eight glass doors, the rest of which were closed. As they turned to walk towards the kiosk to pay for their tickets Lucy saw a pink Nimnad! It was hovering around, staring into space. For a moment she thought it was Nim.... But sadly it wasn't. Having very quickly gotten over the disappointment of it not being HER Nimnad, Lucy felt a little giggle brewing inside her and she guided Sam right through it! POOF! A puff of pink smoke, and it was gone! Now Lucy would stand back and wait patiently to see what Sam's punishment was going to be. She knew it was wrong, but she wanted revenge. They paid for their tickets and bought their own refreshments as agreed. Lucy had a coke, a packet of chewy fruit sweets and Sam had a coke and a hot dog with ketchup and onions. Lucy paid for her stuff and Sam took a ten pound note from his wallet to pay for his. He handed it over and waited for his change. As the girl behind the counter handed him his change he held out his hand to take it. For some unknown reason he totally missed it and dropped his change all over the sweet counter, and what didn't land amongst the sweets, rolled around all over the floor! Lucy could see that Sam was getting very embarrassed and she watched as he sifted through the chocolate bars to find his money. She picked up a few coins from the floor and handed them to him. An embarrassed Sam picked up his coke and hot dog and then they made their way to Screen 2 where the film was showing. Lucy felt a big sense of satisfaction as she inwardly gloated about Sam's misfortune. As they walked along a wide carpeted corridor to Screen 2, Lucy saw another pink Nimnad ahead. There was also a blue one a bit further down the corridor but Lucy chose, with a cheeky little chuckle to herself, to let Sam walk right through the pink one! She waited mischievously for the next bit of bad luck to bestow itself on Sam. AGAIN!!!

They entered the doors to screen 2 and made their way towards the back. They sat themselves down about 2 rows from the back and just beside the aisle so that it was easy to get in and out if they needed to. Lucy took a sip of her drink and placed it in the cup holder which was on the arm of her chair. Sam stood his drink in his cup holder and took a big bite out of his hot dog. As he bit into it, ketchup squirted out from the other end, followed by a stream of onions which slithered down his jacket and landed on his lap. How embarrassing! Sam was beginning to feel really stupid in front of Lucy, who giggled as she unwrapped a sweet and said, "It's not your night is it?" Looking at him like she was about to burst out laughing. She watched as Sam sank deeper into his seat in the hopes that nobody else would be able to see the mess he was in. He wiped off what he could with his serviette as the lights were dimming, and everyone quietened down for the beginning of the film. Even when the lights were dimmed Lucy could still see a couple of faint glows where Nimnads were hovering. There was one in the aisle about four rows back from the front, it was a pink one. There was also a blue one along the adjacent aisle to where they were sitting. Now......, what Lucy should have done was to find a way to get Sam to collide with the blue Nimnad at some point, to make up for all the bad luck he'd just had. That is, if she'd felt any remorse for the way she had been treating him. But she didn't. Not yet anyway! Better still, it would have been good if Lucy had not done anything at all! But, Lucy had that pink Nimnad firmly fixed in her sight and it was slowly moving towards the end of the row of seats and would soon be out in the aisle! She thought hard for an excuse to get Sam to go back to the kiosk for her, in the hope that he would bump into the Nimnad.

"Sam," she whispered.

"Yeah," Sam whispered back to her.

"My throat's really dry. I need a drink of water, could you go and get me a bottle please?" Sam sighed and thought to himself that he didn't REALLY want to move AT ALL until the film ended. Especially after all the accidents he'd been having! But instead of saying what he really felt he wanted to say, which was "No," he found himself saying a polite "yeah, no problem." As he moved from his seat, Lucy could see that he was going to reach the middle of the aisle at the exact same moment as the pink Nimnad! POOF! The Nimnad disappeared......

"Thanks Sam." Lucy said to him as he went to walk away in the direction of the exit. Completely unaware of what Lucy had just let him in for, he just smiled back.

Whilst Sam was gone, Lucy began to feel a little bit guilty as she sat watching the film. As she waited for him to return she started to wonder if she had taken the whole revenge thing a bit too far. Just then, Lucy saw Sam returning from the walkway that led to the exit doors of screen 2. He was carrying her water in one hand and he had a carton of popcorn in the other hand. It was huge! More like a small bucket and Lucy wondered how anyone could ever eat as much popcorn as that single handed!

She watched him as he approached their seats She was looking at him and thinking to herself how fit he was. As she continued to watch him she had the shock of her life!

The poor boy! His foot must have skidded on something slippery, because one of his legs flew up in front of him! He fell backwards and landed on his bum! His popcorn flew up in the air as he slipped over and was landing on him and nearby surrounding people. It was just like watching something on the TV in slow motion! Lucy saw the whole thing in graphic detail! It looked as though it was snowing popcorn all around him. Poor Sam! He retrieved Lucy's bottle of water from where it had landed. All the while, people were applauding and laughing at him. He came back and sat beside Lucy, speechless.

"Sam.... Are you alright?" she asked him.

He nodded in response. He could barely look at her because he was so embarrassed.

"Sorry." she whispered to him.

"I don't know why you're sorry?" he whispered whilst glancing sideways at Lucy. "It wasn't your fault."

NOW Lucy DID feel VERY guilty. She knew she had taken it too far. They both sat quietly watching the film. Neither of of them laughed at the funny bits as neither of them felt like laughing. As the film drew near to the end Lucy began to try to think of ways to make up for treating Sam so badly. He was completely unaware that Lucy had done anything wrong at all, but the fact still remained that SHE knew that her actions had been responsible for the way Sam must be feeling right now, and she really wanted to make him feel better about himself. Although she knew how wrong it was to manipulate the Nimnads so that she got what she wanted, she could see no other quick fix way of making Sam feel happy again. So she decided that when the film was over, she was going to do her upmost to get him into the path of the very next blue Nimnad that she could see.

Very soon the film had finished and people were standing up from their seats, straightening out their clothes and putting coats on ready to leave. You could hear the humming of everyone chatting and laughing about the storyline of the film and comparing their best bits with each other. There was no chatting or laughing going on between Lucy and Sam. He was completely deflated. He had nothing to say and to be honest anyone in Sam's shoes would probably be wishing they could just blink their eyes and be back at home, with the whole ordeal of a disastrous evening behind them!

Lucy stood up and said to Sam, "shall we go then?" He looked up at her, gave a slight smile and nodded. When Lucy stood up she could see that Sam had a couple of sticky bits of popcorn stuck to his dark wavy hair. She just gently picked them off and threw them on the floor. Neither of them said a word about it. Sam stood up and whilst Lucy was putting her jacket on, he was trying to brush the front of his jeans down with a crumpled serviette which he found in his pocket from earlier. There were ketchup stains down the front of his legs but he had to give up because by then it had dried and wasn't going anywhere until the jeans went in the washing machine.

"Come on then," instructed Lucy. Sam looked at her, then turned away to head out of the row of seats where they had been sitting and into the aisle to join the queue of others waiting to make their way out of the exit. Lucy followed closely behind him. Finally after a few minutes it was their turn to leave Screen 2. They squinted as they adjusted their eyes to the bright lights out in the corridor and walked towards the foyer where the kiosk was. There in the foyer, Lucy saw a blue Nimnad! It was faintly glowing, hovering around just outside the entrance to the toilets. It was a faint glow but she could see it and it was DEFINITELY THERE!!!

"OK," thought Lucy. "I've got to act quickly," she told herself. Sam walked right past it! so she grabbed him by the back of his jacket. "Hey, hang on a minute Sam." She said. "I need to pop to the loo." (Pride had to take a backseat on this occasion!) "Can you wait here for me in case I lose you?" she asked him. All Sam wanted to do was go home but he couldn't very well say "no." He inwardly sighed and turned around to walk back to the toilets. He hadn't quite made it as far as the Nimnad and there were quite a few people milling around, some were only just missing it too! There was no time to waste so Lucy had to act quickly again! She pretended to trip as she walked past Sam, and shoved him into the blue Nimnad! In a puff of blue smoke ...., it disappeared!

"Yes it worked!" She shouted to herself in her head.

"Oops sorry," she apologised to Sam, looking embarrassed as she felt a bit silly. He just looked at her with raised eyebrows, although he did feel a bit better about himself, as he was now not the only one to be having clumsy accidents.

All that was left as Lucy walked away in the direction of the ladies toilet was the blue smoke, which of course nobody else could see!

Lucy stood by the sinks in the ladies for a few moments and then washed her hands before going back out to find Sam. He was standing by a grabber machine looking at the prizes inside it. She walked across to him and smiled, he smiled back. For some reason (known only to Lucy) he looked a little brighter and not quite so down.

"You gonna have a go?" she asked him.

"You ARE joking?" he asked her back. "What? after the sort of luck I've had tonight? you MUST be joking." He said as he shook his head and went to turn away from the machine.

"Oh go on. PLEASE." Lucy begged. "Go on Sam? see if you can win one...., for me?" she asked as she pouted her bottom lip out as if to pretend to cry and then they both had to laugh. He took a deep breath and groaned.

"Alright alright," he said as he fished around in his pocket for the right change to put into the machine. It looked as though it was due to be refilled soon which wasn't going to make Sam's job any easier, and the strange thing was that what was left in the machine were fluffy toys about six inches tall. Some were blue and some were pink AND they looked amazingly similar to the Nimnads!

"Oh Sam.......... PLEASE...., can you try to win me a pink one?" Lucy asked him. Sam didn't answer. He put his money in the coin slot and studied the positions of the toys. None of them looked accessible as they were all in very awkward positions and stuck behind each other. The only pink one that looked remotely worth trying for was furthest away from the opening where the grabber would drop the prize out. It was going to be a very slim if not impossible chance of keeping hold of it. That's if he was lucky enough to pick it up in the first place. But, he would try anyway. After the evening he'd had he figured he had nothing to lose and everything to gain. He pushed the start button. The grabber began to move away from him towards the back of the machine. Fairground music was playing loudly from a speaker on the front of the machine below the hand controls. Lucy was jumping up and down to the side of the glass cabinet which was housing the prizes. She was watching the grabber move towards the back of the cabinet.

"STOP!" she shouted, as it looked as though it was in line with the pink fluffy toy. Sam quickly slammed his hand down on the stop button....... He waited for the grabber's claw to settle down and stop swinging around, as the sudden jolt of stopping always made that happen. Then he ran round to the side of the cabinet to where Lucy was standing, he looked to see if he had managed to line it up properly with the prize he was hoping to win for her.

"Yes!" he shouted as he moved quickly back to the front of the machine. The grabber was now stationary.

"NOW!" Lucy shouted. "GO, NOW!" she shouted again as Sam had placed his hand over the grab button, but hesitated to press it. He slammed his hand down again. This time the grabber moved positively across the cabinet in the direction of the pink fluffy toy. By now, Lucy was standing behind Sam, looking over his shoulder in an effort to align her vision with his.

"LET GO! LET GO! LET GO!" she shouted as she was frantically tapping him on the shoulder.
He let go and the grabber immediately dipped down towards the toys beneath it, claws open and outstretched in a bid to pick up anything it could reach in its path. As it reached the level of the toys it began to close.

"PICK UP! PICK UP!" Sam shouted.
Lucy held her breath as she watched excitedly........... For a moment Sam thought he was going to be unlucky, until... Just as the claws had almost completely closed their grasp, one of them managed to slip through a label which was attached to the toy's foot!

"YES!" Lucy shouted. "YOU'VE GOT IT!"

Sam watched with eyes wide open and holding his breath as he waited for the toy to fall off. It swung about from side to to side as the grabber moved towards the opening in the bottom of the cabinet where it came to a jerky halt. The toy had almost become detached from the label. That was the only connection between the toy and the claw! But somehow it managed to hold on by a single thread! Just long enough to reach the opening! Lucy and Sam were entranced as they watched the claw as it swung from left to right above the opening. Both of them now holding their breath and wondering if the now desperately wanted pink fluffy toy would fall back down into the cabinet or if it would fall into the opening and down the plastic chute which lead out of the cabinet and into their hands!

They laughed and cheered with excitement as the toy made a hasty exit from the grabber machine! Sam removed it from the tray underneath the shoot and handed it straight to Lucy.

"Thanks." She said as she smiled sweetly at him, feeling awful about his ordeal with the hot dog and popcorn earlier. She hoped she had been able to make him feel a little bit better, as he definitely seemed to have cheered up now.

"That was so cool. I can't believe I managed to keep hold of that." Sam remarked, feeling rather pleased with himself. "What you gonna call it?" he asked with a cheeky smirk on his face.

"Nim," she answered straight away, without giving it a second thought.

"Nim?" he quizzed Lucy. "Why Nim?"

"Oh...It's, erm... Just that it looks like a Nim." she replied innocently. He shrugged his shoulders and they left the cinema hand in hand. As they walked back towards Lucy's house, they chatted and laughed with each other. Sam even managed to see the funny side of his popcorn accident! When they reached Lucy's house they stopped and stood still, looking at each other. There was a moment of awkwardness and neither of them knew what to do or say. Sam leaned forward and kissed Lucy on the lips.

"Thanks for coming out tonight, I really enjoyed being with you." He said.

"Yeah..... Me too." She replied.

BEING POPULAR

As the next few weeks passed, Lucy became more and more popular at school and Beth's friends became Lucy's friends. Beth began to wander around alone at break time, or sometimes she would stand on the outside of a group of girls trying to participate in their conversation, but nobody really wanted her around. She had gone to great lengths to build her reputation and now it was ensuring that she couldn't make any new friends when she needed to. Suddenly Beth didn't seem so big. Not in size, but in personality. She was of no importance to anyone. She didn't seem so confident and sure of herself and she certainly didn't seem to come across as threatening anymore. Instead, Lucy was strutting around in a very cocky manner. She was making fun of Beth and looking down her nose at people..... People whom only a few weeks ago she would have been grateful just to call her friends.

Friday afternoon arrived much quicker than it usually did. I guess because Lucy was actually quite enjoying her school life now.

Over the coming weeks, she grew increasingly self centered. She was only concerned with herself and her own feelings. She had gathered quite a large group of hangers on, whom Lucy now regarded as her friends. She had discarded Sam, as she had decided that she wasn't ready for a boyfriend yet. After all, there was only space for one important person in Lucy's life and SHE was that person! She was very popular amongst the popular girls, and she could be seen strutting around the playground at break and lunchtime with her newly found friends. She took delight in making fun of less fortunate girls who maybe didn't have trendy enough shoes, or weren't very confident. Her main target though, was Beth. Beth had become surprisingly withdrawn of late and didn't seem to have any particular special friends to hang around with. This was because her friends had found themselves drawn towards Lucy, who was now very self assured, didn't seem to worry about anything and who's mum drove a very flash car which whenever possible, Lucy and her friends would get a lift home from school in!

Of course Lucy oozed confidence! She didn't have to leave anything in life to chance anymore. She could just call upon her Nimnad and manipulate her life as she wanted to. Like the time when the class had just finished a double lesson of outdoor P.E. They had been playing hockey and Lucy was not only content to use her Nimnad to make sure she scored 3 goals but she also made sure that Beth fell face down in a muddy puddle and then the water in Beth's shower ran freezing cold too! Everybody was laughing as Beth screamed out at the shock of the cold shower. Lucy managed to alienate Beth more and more from the other girls.

Nim noticed that Lucy had come to enjoy her new position in school and out of school very much. She had become a girl of great power and influence. She was now someone who looked down on others who may not be as fortunate as herself, whether it be personal looks, fashion or wealth. She was never without a friend who wanted to be by her side and her name was highly respected amongst the other girls at school. OR WAS IT? Maybe the words popular, power and influence were not being used in the right context here? Or respect? Of course all of the previous words quoted are generally good things to 'have' or 'be.' That is, if they've been earned honourably in the right way. But in Lucy's case, she had schemed and cheated her way to the top by using the poor little Nimnad to her own advantage, to the point where she had totally disrespected him. And now she was disrespecting other people around her too. She wasn't friends with Justin or Carley, or any of the other 'popular' people because she LIKED them. She hadn't chosen to make friends with them because she had ANYTHING IN COMMON with them. It was purely a relationship of convenience. They also, were only friends with Lucy because she was now the one to be fearful of. So in short, Lucy had now become a bully! It was the one thing that she despised. The main reason the Nimnad had been sent to her in the first place! And the thing that had caused her so much misery, pain and fear........, SHE had now become. She had no time for the Nimnad anymore, and she practically discarded him. She didn't even bother acknowledging him if she saw him around the house. Nim spent his days and nights sitting alone feeling very sad. He had seen a life very different to the one he had previously known. He had met Lucy and grown very fond of her. He had gone that extra mile to help her and bring some joy back into her life, but sadly he had maybe tried a little too hard and given a little too much. It was no use. Nim decided there was no other way. The only thing he could do now was to call upon the Great Nimnad to ask for his guidance. He waited until Lucy had left to go to school, as he had now become used to being left behind. That is, unless Lucy needed to pass an exam or bake the best cake or even wanted to get her own back on someone! Otherwise she had no use for him. He drifted through the front door, down the path and very sadly he looked back up at Lucy's house, stared for a moment and then turned away and began walking down the road towards the big church. He thought he would wait in a quiet corner of the swing park until after dark. Then he would call upon the Great Nimnad and ask him what he should do about Lucy.

THE GREAT NIMNAD

Nim sat very still under a bush at the edge of the green. He watched the children playing on their bikes and with footballs. As he watched, he noticed a small boy, probably about eight years old. He was standing on his own by the swings, and as he stood there a group of boys ran past, calling him names. Then one of them pushed him over. When the boy stood up Nim could see he was crying and he wondered what it was that made humans behave so badly to each other. He couldn't understand why one person should want to hurt another. In his world everyone was equal.

What had Nim done wrong? How had Lucy gone from being such a sweet, caring, sensitive girl to being so self centred and selfish? Nim hoped that the Great Nimnad would have the answers to his questions.

As night fell and there was nobody left in the park Nim decided that it was time to get the answers he was looking for. He walked into the middle of the grassy area and closed his eyes. As he concentrated hard he radiated a pink glow all around him that shone upwards towards the sky. It looked like pink stardust. Like pink sherbet glistening in the moonlight. Nim sat patiently alone in the dark and waited for the arrival of the Great Nimnad. He didn't know how long that would be but he knew he just had to be patient and wait. There was a growing quietness as the evening turned into night. Fewer cars drove by and there weren't many people walking the streets. Nim thought about how happy he had felt in the beginning when he first met Lucy in her bedroom that night. He pictured the look on her face when she first saw him move. He wanted to smile, but it made him sad to think about the sweet unassuming girl who he had appeared to on that first night, and how they had grown so fond of each other. He had never imagined how helping Lucy to overcome her problems at school would in the end have such a negative effect on her personality. What had he done so wrong? Had he helped Lucy too much? But surely, he thought, "you can't help somebody too much, can you?" he continued to wait, alone in the dark and hope that he would find the answers to his questions.

In the distance, across the grass, Nim noticed a faint golden glow. He watched as the glow became brighter and travelled towards him. The golden shimmery glowing cloud stopped right in front of him. Then it dispersed and faded away to reveal the Great Nimnad. He looked similar to Nim except he was much taller and had thicker and longer golden coloured hair.

Nim stood up as the great Nimnad looked down at him.

"You know it's not often that I am called upon? What is the reason for this visit?" he asked with his deep velvety voice.

"Well," said Nim. "You know you sent me to look after a young girl called Lucy? To bring her some good luck?"

"Yes, go on........." The Great Nimnad seemed a little impatient.

"Well I'm afraid she may have had too much luck now? she's not the same Lucy who I met when I first arrived in her life. In fact I'm afraid that she may be a little more like the people who were upsetting her before I arrived." Nim explained with a worried look on his face.

"Hmmm........ I see," replied the Great Nimnad. "And why do you think that may have happened?"
There was silence as Nim paused and thought deeply for a considerable amount of time. Then he said,

"Well....," in a slightly hesitant voice. "I think Lucy has lost her way and completely forgotten what is truly important." He watched for a reaction, but none came. "I think that she was so relieved from her fear when I arrived in her life that she has..... Erm....Yes.... lost her way." He completed his theory. "Oh yes, I almost forgot....... AND she can see me!" He added urgently, gazing up at the Great Nimnad. Nim wondered if he was cross with him, and if he would somehow blame him for what had happened to Lucy.

The Great Nimnad looked down at Nim in astonishment and said, "She can see you? Well I must say, that has never happened before. You really should have called me before now. This situation is all wrong and should never have been allowed to continue once it was apparent that Lucy could see you." He said disapprovingly.

"There is one very important lesson to be learned in life by every living thing in this world, and that is, that too much of anything can spoil the nicest of people, or the most beautiful animal, or even the most wonderful flower. There is a very fine balance when it comes to the caring and nurturing of any living thing, and that my little Nimnad, is the most important lesson that a parent or guardian of a young one

can learn. We have to develop an understanding.....
An understanding of where the balance is. In Lucy's case, I
fear you may have spoiled her with too much kindness? In
your efforts to avoid disappointment, you have given Lucy too
much luck."

The Great Nimnad realised that Nim had become very
emotionally involved with Lucy, and that wasn't supposed to
be part of the plan. Nimnads aren't supposed to experience
emotions, but Nim had become so close to Lucy that he had
been soaking up her emotions like a sponge. This wasn't good
for a Nimnad. A distraction such as emotion could upset the
balance of luck all over the world! The great Nimnad knew he
had to intervene and do something to help. He looked at the
little pink Nimnad and said, "I think it's best if you don't see
Lucy again."
Nim listened to him, his eyes were staring widely. He could
feel a lump in his throat and he had pools of water
developing in the corners of his eyes, threatening to overflow
and trickle down his face.

"You have tears in your eyes?" the Great Nimnad
wondered how this had happened. He had never known
another Nimnad to cry, other than himself that was.
He'd had a similar experience to the one Nim was having with
Lucy when he was much younger, and that was why he knew
exactly what to do about Nim's situation.

"Can't I at least say goodbye to Lucy?" Nim said quietly.
The tears began to trickle down his face now, winding their
way through his fine pink hair.

The great Nimnad looked sympathetically at Nim again and said. "You may return to Lucy's house one more time only. You may say goodbye to her and explain why you have to leave. Tell her what I have told you about the dangers of losing the balance of life. She will be very upset and sad to see you go. She will beg you to stay, but she WILL understand. And don't be sad. All will be well with Lucy. Your work with her is almost complete." He felt a well of emotion building in himself as he reflected on his own past experiences.

"Don't feel sad. You have done a GOOD job, and next time you will know how to do an even better one. Lucy has lost her way, but you will put it right and she will be ok. You must say goodbye tomorrow."

"Thank you for your help," said Nim as he tried to fight back the tears. The Great Nimnad simply nodded his head and disappeared in a shimmering cloud of golden dust.

Nim walked back to Lucy's house with an aching in his arms and legs and a very heavy heart. The little pink Nimnad was feeling very sad, but tomorrow was a new day and it was going to be the day that he would get the balance between himself and Lucy back where it should be, and that would make him happy.

When Nim arrived back at Lucy's house he could see the lamplight glowing through a gap in the curtains of the front room window. He could see that the landing light was on too. He could hear Buddy sniffing the cold air from behind the front door. Everything looked just the same as it always had done. Except that Nim knew that things were not the same anymore. He knew that tomorrow his and Lucy's lives were going to change again. He was going to say goodbye to her and he didn't really want to. The temperature was dropping and unlike other Nimnads, Nim had learnt how to feel the cold and he began to shiver. He walked around to the side of the house and looked up at Lucy's bedroom window. There wasn't any light coming from it and he thought that it must be quite late in the evening and Lucy was probably in bed. He walked through the garden fence and into Lucy's garden. Then he jumped up onto the garden table and on to the conservatory roof. He walked over to Lucy's window and looked in. It reminded him of the first time he and Lucy met each other. He was peeping through a gap in the curtains and could see Lucy snuggled up in bed fast asleep, just like the first time he saw her. There was a small window open, so the little pink Nimnad climbed through the opening and into Lucy's bedroom. He chose not to drift through the window pane because he wanted to savour every last moment of feeling human as it made him feel closer to Lucy, and he knew that tomorrow it must all come to an end. He gently lowered himself down from the windowsill and crept, ever so quietly, on to Lucy's bed where he curled up at the top of her pillow just above her head. He just wanted to be close to her one more time and to remember all the fun they'd had together. He decided to make himself a promise, and that promise was that he would always remember Lucy no matter what else happened or who else came along. Lucy and Nim had touched each other's lives in a way that no one else could have, and he would never forget that.

A NEW BEGINNING

Morning came far too soon and Nim knew that he had to speak to Lucy about what the future held for both of them. He had to explain to Lucy that it was time to leave her, and the reasons why. He also had to try to make her realise what had happened to her.

Lucy opened her eyes as she woke up. She blinked a few times and then she realised that Nim's little face was looking straight back at her. He had been sitting quietly beside her for quite a while, watching her sleep.

She smiled at Nim and said. "Good morning, my little pink Nimnad."

"Good morning Lucy," he replied.

Only he wasn't smiling because he was feeling very sad inside.

"What's the matter Nim?" Lucy asked. "You don't seem to be your usual happy self."

"No Lucy, that's because I'm not." He replied. "You see, I think we need to talk about the way things have been going at school lately Lucy."

"Well my little Nimnad," Lucy began. "Things are going really well." She said quite excitedly. "I've got plenty of friends now. Even Beth's friends are my friends now, and the best thing about that is that they don't like Beth anymore!" She raised her voice as she was getting more excited.

"It's so funny Nim." she said, getting pretty hyped up. "We make fun of Beth most days at school. Do you remember the day when I messed up her science experiment and she ended up looking like she had just climbed out of a chimney?

Everyone was laughing and she was really upset about it!" laughed Lucy.

Nim had climbed down from Lucy's bed by now and was sitting on the floor looking up at her as she sat on the edge of her bed, enthusiastically telling him how her life had changed.

"Yeah and it's so good now, because I can stick up for myself so no one will mess with me anymore. In fact some people even seem to be scared of me! I think Beth tries to hide if she sees me because she doesn't have any friends now and she's scared of what I might do or say to her! Ha! ha! It's great!" she raised her voice excitedly again.

There was a pause of silence between them. Their eyes met, and for a moment there was a connection that reminded Nim of how it was in the beginning, but it didn't last long because Lucy was soon up and off her bed, bustling around her room and getting ready for school as if she didn't have a care in the world.

"But Lucy," Nim said. "We need to have a talk before you go to school this morning."

"No we don't Nim," she replied. "I'm fine, in fact I'm fantastic and I've never been happier. I don't have any worries, I have friends and I feel good Nim!" she said with a big smile on her face.

"Why do you feel good?" he asked. She paused for a second, thought and said. "Well it's simple.............., everyone wants to be my friend and no one wants to upset me because they know what the result will be, ha ha! And it wouldn't be pretty!" she said as she laughed. Nim stared into Lucy's face as he listened to what she had to say. There was no expression on his little face, he just waited patiently and gave her time to think about what she was saying. "..........What?" she asked him with a puzzled look on her face. He didn't say a word. He just looked at her as tears welled up in his eyes. He fought to keep them from rolling down his face. The lack of Nim's response made Lucy realise that all was not well with him. She wondered if she had said something that had offended him. And then it dawned on her. She re-played the conversation that she'd just had with Nim and it was at that moment that Lucy realised what she'd become. The feeling of pride that she'd had before quickly turned into shame as it engulfed her like a cold wave, starved of oxygen! She drew a short sharp breath and looked at Nim. Their eyes met and there was a connection again.

"OMG! I've turned into Beth, haven't I?" she asked Nim with a look of despair on her face.

"Yes Lucy," he replied. "You have let your good luck go to your head. You have no balance in your life anymore. Last night I had such a feeling of sadness that I met with the Great Nimnad to ask for advice Lucy. He says I will have to leave you now. You don't need me anymore Lucy, I have done my job." Nim paused and swallowed hard as he struggled to speak without showing how upset he really was.

"I'm afraid I have allowed you to have too much of your own way Lucy, which has made you lose your focus on what's really important. It's time for you to draw on your own strength now Lucy and regain your balance so that you can make things right. I've got to leave you now." He just about managed to get his words out without caving in to the emotional strain he was now feeling.

"No you can't." Lucy began to cry "I don't want you to go, please don't leave me Nim. I'm so sorry for being selfish. I'll stop I promise." She sobbed. Nim replied in a soft voice.

"Please don't apologise Lucy. I'm so glad I was able to help you, and you have been on a really important journey. You have learned how it feels to be Lucy, and you have learned how it feels to be someone else. I hope that this experience will help you to find a happy place in your heart." Lucy was determined to find that happy place in her heart, and she realised that Nim was serious when he said he had to leave her. She knelt down to him.

"Thank you Nim," she began. "I have learned so much from my time with you and I will NEVER forget you Nim." She started to cry again.

"And I have also learned from you Lucy." Nim smiled at her. "Please don't cry." He held out his hand towards her. "You are going to be ok, now give me one last hug Lucy. I have to go now." He said. Lucy reached out her arms towards Nim. She was still crying as she went to put her arms around him.

"No..... I can't do it. I don't want you to go Nim." She sobbed.

"You have to do it Lucy....., one last hug."

"I love you Nim and I will never ever forget you." She tried to fight back the tears as she hugged him.

"I will never forget you either Lucy," he replied as he slowly disappeared into a cloud of pink smoke. As he disappeared out of sight, Lucy's arms closed around her own body until she was sitting on the floor hugging nothing but herself. She felt very empty and alone as she sat crying on her bedroom floor. She knew that Nim wasn't going to reappear this time and she owed it to him to pick herself up and sort things out. As difficult as it was, and as much as her heart was aching, she knew she had to begin. She went to the bathroom for a wash and to brush her teeth and on the way back she bumped into Ryan.

"Alright Luce?" he asked.

"Yeah, I s'pose so," she sighed. "Can I walk to school with you today?" she asked him.

"Er...., we don't go to the same school Lucy?" he answered looking confused.

"No I know," she said. "But we could walk some of the way together, couldn't we?"

"Alright then," he said. He wondered what had come over Lucy all of a sudden.

He went downstairs for some breakfast and Lucy returned to her room to finish getting ready for school. She didn't feel much like eating, so when she was ready she ran downstairs to where Ryan was waiting for her in the hallway. They picked up their bags and left the house. Lucy didn't even say goodbye to her mum. As they started to walk down the road Lucy said that she had something to tell Ryan.

"What's up Lucy?" he asked.

"Well. You know the Nimnad?"

"Your imaginary friend, you mean?" he asked her.

"Hmm..., well he's gone." she said.

"Oh ok, is that it?" Ryan flippantly said, as he'd not believed her in the first place! Lucy and Ryan walked the rest of their time together in silence. Ryan didn't show any interest in what she was about to tell him so she sulked in silence for the rest of their journey together. She wished she'd appreciated Nim more, even when she had got used to him being around. She longed to see him by her side. When it was time, Lucy and Ryan said their goodbyes and went their separate ways. It had been a very long time since Lucy had felt this low. She thought long and hard as she walked the rest of the way to school, and she had to smile as she remembered the first time she ever saw Nim's face staring straight back at her as she lay in her bed. She reminisced about the fun times they'd had together, and then she thought about how sad he looked when he'd had to leave her. Lucy knew that she owed it to Nim, if not herself, to rebalance her life. She decided right then and there that she was going to make a change at school. She was going to become friends with Beth AND remain friends with everyone else too!

Lucy arrived at school where her friends were ready to greet her. They welcomed her like bees round a honey pot, waiting for the next entertaining episode between her and Beth. Little did they know that they were ALL about to experience a change in life balance due to the Nimnad.

"Hi Lucy," said one girl. "Alright Lucy?" another called out. Another greeted her with a hug and a kiss. She certainly wasn't short of company these days! Lucy stood with her friends, laughing and joking whilst they waited for the bell to ring before everyone made a mad dash for their classrooms.

Beth sat alone on a step in a doorway, which had become usual for her. She was drinking hot chocolate which she'd bought from the breakfast bar as she did every morning. Without a word to anyone, Lucy started walking across to where Beth was sitting. The group of friends she'd been standing with followed and watched in anticipation of what would happen next. Beth was looking at Lucy and then looking at her feet intermittently. She wasn't sure what to do or where to look, OR what was going to happen. Her stomach knotted up, her mouth went dry and she felt as though she wanted to throw her hot chocolate on the floor and run away. But instead, her body froze on the spot where it sat. Lucy had known that feeling all too well! She had made her way over to Beth now and was standing in front of her looking down at where she was sitting.

"Alright?" Lucy asked Beth.

Everyone was puzzled. What would Lucy do next? She was obviously lulling Beth into a false sense of security and then she was going to do something mean to her they thought. Beth stared into her cup of hot chocolate.

"Alright?" Lucy asked again.

That time Beth slowly looked up at Lucy very nervously and answered.

"Yeah." She was waiting for Lucy to come back at her with a sarcastic remark or some kind of nasty behaviour. How wrong she was. Lucy simply nodded her head in acknowledgement of Beth's answer, and walked away. Everyone was confused, including Beth.

"What was that all about?" Beth wondered.
Obviously the punch line would come later..... But it didn't.
The day passed peacefully without any nasty remarks from
Lucy. No pranks, or stunts were pulled on anyone in Lucy's
path. She just went about her business quietly, did her lessons
and walked quietly home at the end of the day. Lucy's new
friends were wondering what was wrong with her. It seemed
like she was there in person, but her mind was somewhere
else. Beth felt very un-nerved as she walked briskly home
from school, frequently looking over her shoulder in case
anyone was creeping up behind her. Although it was such a
relief to have made it through a whole school day without
some form of humiliation or torment, it was also strangely
unsettling as she'd now grown used to the misery and felt
jumpy and nervous because she was waiting for something to
happen.... But nothing did. Beth arrived home and there she
stayed until the next morning, as she always did since her
friends had become Lucy's friends. She didn't have anyone
to go anywhere with anymore and she didn't feel comfortable
going out alone. She only went out alone if she really had to,
like walking to and from school.

Lucy arrived home. There wasn't anybody indoors yet so
she poured herself a glass of orange juice and took it upstairs
to her room. She kicked off her shoes and pushed them to
the foot of her bed, put her glass of orange juice on her
bedside cabinet and threw her blazer onto her bed. Then she
slumped, cross legged onto her bed, leaning back against
the wall. She picked up her remote control and switched on
the TV. She began to to play on her Xbox. It still had the

same game in it that she'd been playing when Nim had been with her. She remembered how he had watched with great interest and asked what it was. Her fingers were pushing the buttons on the controls but her mind was on the little pink Nimnad. She was wondering where he was now and what he was doing. She really wished she could see him again and tell him how much she loved him and how grateful she was for everything he'd done for her. Then her attention turned to the last conversation they'd had before he left. She thought about what she had told him about her new friends and her new power. She thought about how the Nimnad had entered her life and then she thought about Beth. Lucy could see everything so clearly now. She felt ashamed of herself and she couldn't believe how blind she had been to what she was doing.

The next day Lucy woke up earlier than usual, her head full of what she wanted to do from now on, and the changes she wanted to make. She wanted to speak to Beth and find out what she was really like. She wanted to remain friends with her new friends and for them to like her for who she really was, but what she wanted more than anything was to make a difference. Once she was washed and ready for school she went downstairs for something to eat and drink. Mum was by the kettle pouring out some tea.

"Do you want a cup love?" she asked.

Lucy sat at the table and looked at her mum. She looked the same as she always did. She was the same mum, but something was different. Today Lucy could really SEE her mum. She could really see who her mum was and for the first time in ages she appreciated her.

"Yes please mum. Thanks." Lucy said.

Ryan walked into the kitchen and started putting some cereals into a bowl for himself.

He didn't bother to speak to Lucy because she was usually too grumpy first thing in the morning to want to speak to anyone.

"Morning Ryan." She greeted him with a smile on her face.

Ryan looked at his sister with suspicion in his eye and said, "yeah...., good morning."

"Toast love?" asked Lucy's mum.

"That would be lovely. Thanks mum." she replied. She checked the time on her watch and took a slice of toast with her to eat on the way to school.

Bye mum! See you later Ryan!" She called out from the front door. Dad had already left for work before Lucy and Ryan had woken up.

Lucy arrived at school earlier than usual. None of the little group of girls who were normally waiting for her were there yet. She thought that Beth might be in the canteen, so she headed for the breakfast bar and went in to have a look. There was a scattering of girls in there. Two or three small groups and half a dozen girls sitting alone. All were eating and drinking and chatting or texting on their mobile phones.

Beth was sitting alone at the far end of the canteen. Lucy knew that's where she would be because she used to do the same thing. She walked over to where Beth was sitting. Beth didn't look up even though she could sense that Lucy was standing beside her. Beth's stomach began to tie up in knots again, her palms became cold and clammy and she couldn't think straight. Lucy sat down beside her and Beth glanced sideways, but still didn't look up. She pretended to be even more engrossed in her magazine than she already had been.

"Alright Beth?" Lucy asked.

"Yeah," replied Beth, feeling very nervous.
The two of them sat in silence for a moment.

"Look...., what do you want?" Beth asked, having finally plucked up the courage to speak to Lucy. Her arms and legs tingled, her neck froze and she felt sick in her stomach again. She was frightened and Lucy could see it.

"What do YOU want Beth?" asked Lucy.

"What do you mean, what do I want?" She answered, sounding really fed up. "I want my mates back, I want to be left alone..........." Beth was still speaking as Lucy interrupted her.

"You want to walk down the road feeling comfortable. You want to feel happy, and You want to stop feeling sick in the pit of your stomach. I'm right aren't I Beth?" Then she continued before Beth could answer. "You want to be able to look people in the eye and smile without wondering what they will do or say to you. And you don't want to feel terrified when somebody speaks to you..., so scared that your mouth dries up and you can't speak back." Lucy completed her statement.

Beth stared at Lucy and said nothing. Her eyes welled with tears.

"I know." Lucy said. "Because it's how I used to feel every day from Monday to Friday, that's how I felt. The weekends were a little bit better but only because I could go out with my mum or dad and I knew no one could hurt me if I was with them. But I still felt the same inside." Beth continued to stare at Lucy in silence. The tears overflowed and began to trickle down her face.

"Sorry," she said. She was thinking as she gazed into her hot chocolate. "I bullied you didn't I?"

"Yeah Beth, you did." Lucy told her. "And now I am a bully," she said, looking deep into Beth's face and realising how alike they actually probably were.

It was nearly time for the bell to go and during the time that Lucy had been with Beth in the canteen, everyone else had been arriving at school. Lucy's friends were in the playground and had assumed that Lucy was absent from School as they hadn't seen her.

"I wish I had never bullied you Lucy." Beth said, as she pushed her cup of hot chocolate to one side. She didn't feel much like drinking it now.

"So do I." Lucy replied. "And now YOU know what it is like to be bullied, and I know what it's like to be the bully."

They both agreed that being on the wrong side of a bully is the most horrible experience they'd ever known. They also agreed that, having both been bullied that there was no pride or power in being a bully. They realised that it took a lot more courage to be yourself rather than trying to 'be popular', and that having friends who like you for WHO you you are and not WHAT you are was far more rewarding. They also understood the true meaning of friendship now and why it was so important to be a friend and not just have them. They decided to leave the canteen together when the bell rang, and they also realised that they actually did like each other! They wanted to become friends. It was very confusing for all concerned when Beth and Lucy emerged from the canteen, smiling and talking to each other!

"Alright?" Lucy greeted her little group as she walked over to them.

"Alright?" Beth greeted the same group as she walked over to them as well. The group of girls all looked at each other with a puzzled expression on their faces and then they all looked at Lucy and Beth. Lucy and Beth looked at the group and then at each other and burst out laughing. They didn't feel the need for explanations to anyone about their actions, and they just blended their way into the group. Gradually everyone accepted the situation and settled down. Finally, life really did feel good. Lucy was truly happy AND so was Beth. They became very good friends and by the end of the school year there was a very good balance in Lucy's group of friends. Nobody was the boss and they all liked and respected each other for the individuals they were.

Summer had arrived and so had the holidays. Lucy and her friends celebrated by going to the park for a water fight. They met some of the boys from Ryan's school too. Ryan was there with some of his friends and they all had a great time together. Lucy and Beth became best friends during those summer holidays. In fact Lucy's mum and dad even invited Beth to go away with them. Sometimes the two girls would remember how things used to be and then they would shake their heads and laugh in disbelief.

Finally, it was the end of the holidays and the new school term began. Lucy had two more years at school and would be studying very hard for her GCSE's. She arranged to meet Beth at the school gates on the first day back and Beth was waiting there for her when she arrived. They looked at each other smiled and said "Alright?" Then they laughed as they linked arms and walked into school.

There were a lot of new girls starting too. The new year sevens. They were dotted around in little groups, chatting to each other. Some looked excited, some were laughing and some looked positively terrified. As Lucy and Beth looked around observing them all they both noticed a girl who was standing alone by the canteen. She looked very awkward, as though she didn't know what to do with her feet and didn't seem to find it very easy to look anybody in the eye. Lucy and Beth looked at each other and shrugged their shoulders. The bell rang and they went inside to their classroom. That day passed amidst a sea of new books and timetables. There was also a list of new teacher's names to familiarise themselves with. The next day they met as usual at the school gates and went in. They noticed the same girl standing alone, but this time there was a small group of girls standing nearby making fun of her. They were calling her silly names and embarrassing her. She was clearly very intimidated and was looking down at her feet. She looked like she might cry. Lucy and Beth looked at each other and shook their heads in disapproval. This time they couldn't ignore it.

"No way," they both said at the same time. They walked off to find their mates Justine, Carley, Kerry and Amber. They explained to them what was going on and said, "come on girls. We're going to stop this." They were very determined. The six of them made their way across the playground towards where the girl was still standing. She was looking very anxious and the other girls were standing right in front of her. They were pointing at her shoes and making sarcastic comments about them because they weren't as trendy as the ones that they were all wearing. Lucy, Beth and the others marched over to them and pushed their way through.

"Is there a problem here?" Beth asked them.

"Yeah, is there?" Lucy joined in. "What's going on?" she asked. The younger girls looked surprised at the intervention of Lucy and her friends. They couldn't think of anything to say in their defence. The girl who had been standing alone looked surprised too.

"You ok?" Lucy asked her. The girl nodded her head but didn't say anything. Beth checked out the group of girls and spoke to the one who looked most likely to be the ring leader.

"Have you got a problem with this girl?"

"No." She replied.

"Then, what are you doing?" Lucy asked.

"Yeah...., why are you bullying her?" Carley piped up. The girls looked offended at having been called bullies! They stuttered for an answer but couldn't think of one.

"Look," said Lucy. "We know what you're doing and it's not gonna happen. You might as well give up now because we don't have bullying in our school."

"Yeah," said Beth. "We don't like bullies." She paused. "So you might as well give up now or you could end up getting some of your own treatment."
The group very sheepishly turned and walk away. The young girl looked at Lucy and smiled shyly.

"What's your name?" Lucy asked her.

"Katie." she quietly replied in a timid voice.

"Do you want to come and stand with us?"
Katie nodded. Nobody ever bothered her again. From that day until the girls left the school, they looked out for anyone who seemed unhappy or who was being picked on, and they gradually stamped bullying out of their school. Things at school changed a lot for Lucy and her life began to get back

on track. The friendship that Lucy and Beth had formed between themselves deepened until they got to the stage where there was trust and loyalty on both sides and for the first time in a long while, Lucy was truly happy again. Beth had also discovered how nice it was to be genuinely liked for who she was and NOT what she was or what she represented. The two girls would regularly go clubbing and often took Buddy for a walk together. They had become great friends, both of them with a clear understanding of what true friendship meant and how it felt to walk in someone else's shoes.

One Sunday afternoon Lucy decided to take Buddy to the park for a run. She text Beth from her mobile to see if she wanted to go too, and arranged to meet her there, as Beth was just finishing dinner with her family.

Lucy arrived at the park and let Buddy off his lead. She sat down on a bench under some trees to wait for Beth. The weather was a bit chilly and there was quite a strong wind blowing, so she sat there for a bit of shelter. As she waited she looked around the park. There was a couple with a toddler over the other side of the park, near the lake. They were laughing as they pushed their little one along in a buggy. They looked like they were having fun. There were a few children in the playground area. A couple were on the slide, and a few were wandering around, trying to decide what to play on next whilst their parents sat nearby chatting to each other. In the distance Lucy could see Beth crossing the road and making her way over towards the park gates.

Lucy stood up and called Buddy to come back to her. He had been leisurely walking around sniffing at the trees and grass. She clipped his lead back onto his collar and started to walk towards Beth. They met in the middle, quite near to the playground.

"Hi Beth, alright?"

"Yeah, you? what you been up to?" Beth asked.

"Well.....," and just as Lucy was about to answer her, Buddy started barking and jumping around like crazy.

"Sit down Buddy!" Lucy shouted at him.

Buddy did sit down but he was staring up at Lucy, panting frantically.

"What's up with him?" Beth asked.

"I don't know?" Lucy answered, shrugging her shoulders. She knelt down in front of him and began stroking his head. Suddenly, he stopped panting and paused for a moment. Then Lucy heard,

"ACHOO!"

She turned and looked behind her, but nothing. Beth asked her if she was alright.

"Erm..., yes....., I think so. Did you hear anything just then?"

"No," replied Beth. "Like what?"

"Like a sneeze?" suggested Lucy.

"No," Beth giggled. "You sure you're feeling alright?" she asked Lucy, still laughing.

"Yes, I think so," Lucy said as they began to walk.

"ACHOO!"

Lucy heard it again! She smiled as she looked around. She couldn't see him, but she knew he must be nearby. She would have recognised that sneeze anywhere! Just knowing that he was still around made Lucy a very happy girl.

THE END!

Printed in Great Britain
by Amazon